A Deadly Call

"Hello, Johanna?" a boy's voice said.

"Yes. Who's this?" I didn't recognize the voice.

"It's Dennis. Dennis Arthur."

I nearly gasped into the phone. I was so startled. Dennis was calling *me?*

"Hi, Dennis," I managed to choke out. "You're back from vacation?"

"Yeah. This morning," he replied. And then he lowered his voice to just above a whisper. "Hey, Johanna," he murmured, "are you ready to kill Mr. Northwood?"

Books by R. L. Stine

Available from ARCHWAY Paperbacks

FEAR STREET®
R·L·STINE

The Dare

A Parachute Press Book

AN ARCHWAY PAPERBACK
Published by POCKET BOOKS

New York   London   Toronto   Sydney   Tokyo   Singapore

AN ARCHWAY PAPERBACK *Original*

An Archway Paperback published by
POCKET BOOKS, a division of Simon & Schuster Inc.
1230 Avenue of the Americas, New York, NY 10020

Copyright © 1994 by Parachute Press, Inc.

ISBN: 0-671-73870-4

First Archway Paperback printing February 1994

10 9 8 7 6 5 4 3 2 1

FEAR STREET is a registered trademark of Parachute Press, Inc.

AN ARCHWAY PAPERBACK and colophon are registered trademarks of Simon & Schuster Inc.

Cover art by Bill Schmidt

Printed in the U.S.A.

IL 7+

prologue

Am I really doing this?

The question repeated in my mind as I made my way across the backyard.

The pistol in my hand felt hot, as if it were about to burst into flame.

Am I really doing this?

Do I really have a loaded pistol in my hand?

Am I really going to use it?

Johanna Wise, murderer.

Is that how I will be known from now on?

"She was always a quiet girl. Rather mousy." That's how the neighbors will describe me in the newspaper. "She lived with her divorced mother. They didn't have much money. Johanna never seemed to have many friends. But she always had a nice smile for everyone. Who would ever guess?"

Who would ever guess that Johanna Wise was a murderer?

Or maybe I'm not.

Maybe I'm not creeping across to the next yard to kill my teacher.

I mean, would I really kill my teacher just because of a stupid dare?

Maybe this is just another one of my fantasies.

I have so many violent fantasies these days. I imagine so many frightening things.

Maybe this is another fantasy.

My stomach really hurts. This is the worst stomach-ache I've ever had.

My hand is sweating.

I'm really afraid.

Am I really doing this?

Yes. I am.

I'm raising the pistol.

I'm squeezing the trigger.

Once I kill him, I'll feel so much better.

chapter
1

I guess it started weeks ago at the 7-Eleven. The one at the end of Mission Street, way past the mall.

It was a little after eight o'clock. A cold, clear night. I remember thinking the stars overhead looked a little like snowflakes.

My best friend, Margaret Rivers, and I drove to the 7-Eleven in Margaret's little white Geo to get hot dogs. Believe it or not, that was my dinner.

You see, Mom's been working two jobs ever since she and Dad got divorced. She works late every night. Sometimes I don't see her for days. I can't remember the last time the two of us sat down to have dinner together.

So Margaret and I were at the front counter, ordering hot dogs. I was starving. Everyone thinks I don't eat much, because I'm so skinny, but that just isn't true.

Margaret and I don't look like we have a thing in common. But maybe that's why we're such good friends. I'm short and very thin. I've got long, straight black hair—my best feature—and dark brown eyes. My nose is too pointy, and I hate the cleft in my chin—but that's another story.

Margaret is nearly a head taller than I am and kind of chunky. She's still trying to lose her baby fat— that's what she always says. She has curly carrot-colored hair and a face full of freckles. She isn't very pretty, but she's a great friend and she can always make me laugh.

This winter, after my parents' divorce and all, I really needed a friend who could make me laugh. I've always had a tendency to look on the dark side.

You know how people can see a glass of water, and some will say it's half full and someone else will say it's half empty? Well, I'm the kind of person who will say the glass is half empty and cracked, and who cares about a stupid glass of water anyway?

I get depressed a lot. I admit it.

That's why it's so great to have a close friend like Margaret Rivers.

Margaret and I may not have the coolest clothes or drive the best cars. We're both totally broke most of the time, but we manage to have fun sometimes, even in a little town like Shadyside.

"We're out of mustard," the salesclerk at the 7-Eleven said, holding our two hot dogs out to me over the counter. He was a middle-aged man, balding in front, his stomach bulging under his green knit shirt.

"I guess we'll have them plain," I told him.

"I guess," he muttered. He handed over the hot dogs, then threw two more raw dogs on the machine.

"Hey, Johanna—look." Margaret held her hot dog in one hand. She nudged me with the other hand.

I followed her gaze to the back of the store.

I heard laughing and loud voices, and then I saw a bunch of kids I recognized. "What are *they* doing here?" I whispered to Margaret.

There were five kids back there around the Slurpy machine. I didn't know any of them very well— they're seniors and Margaret and I are juniors—but I recognized them right away because Margaret and I have been taking some senior classes.

They were just about the wealthiest kids at Shadyside High. I was sure all five of them lived in North Hills, the ritziest part of town. You know. Enormous houses. Well-kept lawns. Tall hedges to keep riffraff like Margaret and me from getting too close.

They were laughing a lot and shoving one another, knocking the Slurpy cups on the floor. You know, just goofing on each other, having fun.

I saw Dennis Arthur and his girlfriend, Caitlin Munroe. I like Dennis. We're in advanced math together, and he let me copy from his paper during a test once.

He's a pretty good guy. And really great-looking. He's got short black hair and green eyes. He's the star of the Shadyside track team, and he really looks like an athlete.

5

A girl named Melody Dawson was there too. She's a real stuck-up snob. She was kidding around with Lanny Barnes and Zack Hamilton.

Zack is a big guy, built like a wrestler. He has curly red hair and wears bright blue sunglasses day and night. He was bragging in class about how he's related to one of the Founding Fathers, Alexander Hamilton. Maybe it's true. I don't know.

And do I care? No.

I took a bite of my hot dog. It was cold. Margaret and I watched the five kids, trying to look like we weren't watching them.

"I dare you," I heard one of them say. I think it was Lanny.

"I *double*-dare you!" one of them shot back.

Dennis started to pour some of the purple Slurpy stuff into a cup, and Lanny punched the cup out of his hand. The purple slush poured onto Dennis's white sneakers.

"Hey—!" Dennis playfully punched Lanny on the shoulder.

Then Lanny poured a big glob of slush into his hand and shook hands with Dennis.

Margaret and I had to laugh. I mean, it was really funny. But out of the corner of my eye, I saw that the store clerk had an angry scowl on his face. He was getting really steamed.

The Slurpy fight was getting a little wild.

Caitlin and Melody were splashing cups of purple slush at each other. A big glob fell onto Melody's head and trickled down her perfect blond hair.

Dennis started laughing a high-pitched hyena laugh.

But he stopped when Zack and Lanny both dumped cups of the purple stuff down the front of his maroon and gray Shadyside High jacket.

The five kids were slipping and sliding now. The floor was covered with puddles of purple slush. Lanny went down. He hit the floor and slid onto his back. And then Zack sprawled on top of him. Dennis let out that high-pitched laugh again.

Everyone was laughing. Margaret and me too. It was such a riot.

"Stop it right now! I'll call the cops! I really will!"

The clerk's angry shout made everyone stop laughing. I turned and saw that his face was nearly as purple as the Slurpy slush, and the veins were bulging at the sides of his neck. It looked like his head was going to explode. Really.

At the back of the store, Lanny had climbed to his feet. But Zack was still sprawled on the floor. The Slurpy machine was running. The purple slush poured out in a thick stream onto the linoleum.

Dennis tried to help Zack up, but Zack only pulled him to the floor. And everyone started laughing all over again.

"You kids think you can do whatever you like!" the red-faced clerk was shrieking. He burst out from behind the counter, shaking his fist at them.

Oh, no, I thought, glancing warily at Margaret. Is he going to *fight* them?

This was getting intense.

Margaret grabbed my arm. I don't think she even realized she was holding on to me.

The store clerk lumbered over to the five kids, his

stomach heaving as he walked. He was breathing really hard and still shaking his fist angrily. "I'm calling the cops! I'm calling them right now!"

Dennis and Zack climbed to their feet. Melody and Caitlin suddenly had frightened looks on their faces.

"No, you're not," Dennis said quietly.

"Huh? What did you say?" the clerk screamed furiously.

"I said you're not calling the cops," Dennis replied calmly.

And then I saw the gun in Dennis's hand.

Margaret must have seen it too, because her grip tightened on my arm.

I didn't have time to cry out or anything.

"You're not calling anyone," Dennis told the clerk coldly.

And then he pulled the trigger.

chapter

2

A stream of water sprayed from the gun. It splashed onto the front of the store clerk's green shirt.

The kids all went bananas, laughing wildly and slapping each other high-fives.

"Dennis, you're the man!" Lanny cried gleefully. "You're the man!"

The store clerk was so angry, I thought I could see steam rising up from his bald head.

Margaret and I were still huddled together in the front of the store. We were laughing pretty hard too.

There was a pay phone against the back wall. The clerk angrily grabbed the receiver. He pulled it so hard, I thought he was going to jerk the phone off the wall.

"I'm calling the cops," he said in an angry growl.

But then Zack reached for his wallet. I saw him take some bills from it, and he stuffed them into the clerk's shirt pocket. "This should pay for the Slurpys," he said. "And the mess."

And then the five kids paraded past us, big, pleased grins on their faces, and headed out the glass door to the parking lot.

"Just because they're rich, they think they can get away with anything," the store clerk muttered. He was looking down at the big puddles of purple slush.

"Is he talking to us or to himself?" Margaret whispered.

I shrugged.

They went by so fast, I wasn't sure if the Shadyside kids had seen Margaret and me. But I glanced out the front window—and caught Dennis Arthur staring in at me.

That's weird, I thought, feeling my face grow hot.

Why is he staring at me with that weird grin on his face?

I was trying to decide whether to wave to him or not. But before I could decide, his girlfriend, Caitlin, pulled him away.

Mr. Northwood, my history teacher, is tall and very lean. He kind of stoops his head and his shoulders all the time, as if he doesn't really want to be as tall as he is. He has thick, wavy hair. I think it used to be brown, but now it's mostly gray. He has watery blue eyes and a craggy face with lots of deep lines running down his cheeks.

He sort of looks like a beardless Abe Lincoln or maybe Clint Eastwood on a really bad day.

He's a weird guy.

For one thing, he always wears turtlenecks. Never any other kind of shirt or sweater. It's not the most flattering style for him because he has a big, bulging Adam's apple that always bobs up and down right where the turtleneck ends.

Another weird thing about Mr. Northwood is that he tape-records everything. Really. Everything. He has this little silvery mini-recorder that he carries in his pocket.

When class begins, he sets the recorder on the desk and clicks it on. When he's ready to dismiss the class, he clicks off the recorder, removes the tiny cassette, and slips it back into his pocket.

Weird, huh?

The other weird thing about having Mr. Northwood as a teacher is that he's also my next-door neighbor. On Fear Street. But let's not get into that now.

The afternoon after the 7-Eleven incident, I was sitting near the back of my history class, half listening to Mr. Northwood, half daydreaming. I kept glancing at the clock above Mr. Northwood's head. The school day was almost over.

Outside the windows the sky was gray and growing darker. I wondered if it was cold enough to snow. I hoped not. I remembered that I had lost my red wool gloves somewhere, and I didn't have any money to buy another pair.

When Mr. Northwood clicked off his little tape recorder and slid it into his pocket, I sat up straight and began shoving my Trapper Keeper into my backpack.

"Dismissed," Mr. Northwood said in his reedy, thin voice.

I jumped to my feet, straightening the bottom of my white cotton sweater, pulling it down over my faded denims. I left my backpack on the floor, told Margaret I'd meet her in the hall, and started to the front of the room.

I had to ask Mr. Northwood a question about the paper I was writing about Charles Lindbergh. I didn't know if he wanted me just to write about Lindbergh's career, or did I have to write about the kidnapping of his baby too?

I had started to the front when I saw that Dennis Arthur had gotten there first. Mr. Northwood said something to him, and Dennis reacted angrily.

I stopped short as they started to argue.

The room had emptied out. I took a step back, then another, lingering against the wall.

"I *told* you why I can't take the midterm exam!" Dennis cried shrilly. He was gesturing excitedly with his hands. Even from the back of the room, I could see his green eyes flash excitedly. I could tell Dennis was really upset.

"My family always goes to the Bahamas in February," Dennis said, crossing his arms in front of his navy blue sweatshirt. "What am I supposed to do, Mr. Northwood—stay home so I can take your exam?"

Mr. Northwood shook his head. The lines in his

face seemed to grow deeper. "Have a good trip," he said dryly. "Send me a postcard, Dennis."

"Well, I don't see why you can't give me a makeup test when I get back," Dennis insisted, leaning over the teacher's desk, challenging him. "Or give me a test I can take along with me."

Mr. Northwood shook his head, his colorless lips forming the word *no*.

"Why not?" Dennis demanded.

"It would be unfair to your classmates," the teacher replied softly, stooping his head, as always, as he gathered his books and papers together.

I was starting to feel embarrassed listening to this. I mean, I didn't want Dennis to think I was deliberately eavesdropping or anything.

But I don't think Dennis even knew I was in the room. And I really did want to ask Mr. Northwood my question.

So I stayed, leaning against the wall, thinking about how great-looking Dennis is, imagining what it would be like to be Caitlin, his girlfriend, and listening as the argument grew really intense.

"If I get an F, do you know what will happen to me?" Dennis cried. He didn't wait for Mr. Northwood to answer. "I'll lose my eligibility on the track team."

"I feel bad about that," Mr. Northwood replied. As Dennis got louder, the teacher's voice became softer. "I really do, Dennis."

"But all my other teachers are giving me a break!" Dennis exclaimed. "They know I'm going to be all-state this year. They know I could get an Olympics tryout. I could be a national star, Mr. Northwood. I really could."

"I hope so," Mr. Northwood replied, turning his head to glance up at the clock.

"Great! Then give me a makeup test. Give me a break, okay?" Dennis pleaded, staring hard into the teacher's watery eyes.

"In my opinion, you get too many breaks," the teacher replied quietly. He began shoving books into his worn leather briefcase. After a few moments he stopped and raised his eyes to Dennis. "Give me one good reason why I should give you special treatment."

"Because I *asked* you to!" Dennis replied without hesitating.

The room suddenly grew darker as the storm clouds lowered over the sky. One of the overhead fluorescent lights near the door buzzed and flickered.

"Our discussion is over. I'm really sorry," Mr. Northwood told Dennis. He clicked his briefcase shut.

Dennis just gaped at him. His mouth dropped open, but he didn't say anything. Then Dennis threw up his hands in a gesture of total exasperation. "I—I don't believe this!" Dennis screamed, losing his temper.

Suddenly I realized someone was calling my name.

I turned to the door and saw Margaret motioning to me.

As I made my way to Margaret, I could hear Dennis shouting furiously at Mr. Northwood.

"Margaret—what is it?" I whispered, stepping into the doorway.

And then I heard a loud *thud*.

I heard Mr. Northwood let out a cry.

A heavy feeling of dread shot through my body.

Without looking, I knew that Dennis had slugged him.

chapter

3

My breath caught in my throat. I turned back to the front of the room.

I was relieved to see that Dennis hadn't hit Mr. Northwood. He had angrily slammed a heavy textbook to the floor instead.

Mr. Northwood had been calm and soft-spoken, but now he really lost his cool. He went all white and pointed a shaky finger at Dennis and started sputtering at him about respect for school property.

Dennis looked totally stunned. I think he was really upset that he lost his temper like that. He was breathing hard, glaring at Mr. Northwood, balling and unballing his fists as the teacher laced into him.

"What's going on?" Margaret whispered, peeking in timidly from the hall.

"World War Three," I whispered back, picking up my backpack and edging out of the room.

"Who's winning?" Margaret asked as I joined her in the hall.

"Mr. Northwood, I think," I replied, crossing the empty hall to my locker.

I could hear Dennis and Mr. Northwood arguing loudly back in the classroom. I realized my knees were kind of shaky. Why am *I* upset? I wondered. It isn't *my* argument.

No one has offered to take *me* to the Bahamas this February, I thought bitterly. Why should I care if Dennis gets a makeup test or not?

"I'm late for my job," Margaret said, shifting her backpack over her red down jacket. Margaret waitresses at Alma's Coffeeshop for a few hours after school every day. "I just wanted to ask if you want to come to dinner tonight."

"I guess," I said, twirling the combination lock on my locker and pulling the door open. "My mom won't be home till after nine. Thanks, Margaret."

"Later," she called, hurrying down the hall, her red hair bouncing as she ran.

I bent down and started pulling books from my locker and stuffing them into my backpack. A few seconds later, I glanced up to see Dennis angrily stomping out of Mr. Northwood's room.

He crossed the hall, shaking his head, muttering to himself. "I could kill that guy," he said breathlessly to me. "I really could."

I laughed. I didn't know what else to do.

My heart started pounding. I mean, Dennis's locker was two down from mine. But he had never said a word to me before.

I stood up and tried to flash him an encouraging smile. I don't think he noticed. He slammed his fist into his locker door. The *clang* echoed down the hall.

"Ow," I said. "Didn't that hurt?"

"Yeah," Dennis replied. He grinned at me and shook his hand. "It hurt a lot. Stupid, huh?"

"Well . . ." I couldn't think of a good reply. My mouth had gone all dry. Dennis was just so good-looking. I guess I'd had kind of a crush on him for a long time. But I never really allowed myself to think about it.

"I just hate that guy," Dennis grumbled, flexing his hand.

"He isn't being very fair," I said.

"He's a jerk," Dennis replied angrily. "A total jerk." His green eyes locked on my face. It was as though he were seeing me for the first time.

"I could kill him. Really," Dennis repeated. He turned away from me and started fiddling with his combination lock. "You know how?"

"How?" I asked a little too eagerly.

"I don't know," Dennis said, scowling.

"Well, let's see," I replied, thinking hard. "You could glue that little tape recorder to his ear and make him listen to all the classes he records. That would *bore* him to death." I snickered.

Dennis didn't smile. "Not painful enough," he grumbled. He tugged at the locker door, but it wouldn't open. He let out a frustrated groan and started furiously twirling the lock again.

Suddenly he stopped and turned to me. "I'd like to stuff him into that briefcase he always carries," he said. "And lock it shut. And toss it in the trash."

"He's too tall," I replied. "He wouldn't fit."

"I'd fold him up," Dennis said. "That would be the fun part. Folding him."

"Yuck!" I made a disgusted face. "You're really sick."

"No. Just angry" Dennis sighed. "He's going to mess up my life. He really is."

"Well, maybe you should just shoot him," I joked.

"Not as much fun as folding him up first," Dennis replied. He wasn't smiling. I stared at him, trying to determine just how serious he was.

I mean, I knew he couldn't *really* be serious about killing Mr. Northwood.

"You could fold him up and *then* shoot him," I suggested.

Dennis's eyes lit up.

I think Dennis likes me, I thought. He keeps staring at me, studying me with his eyes.

"I could fold him up, shoot him, then *drown* him!" Dennis exclaimed.

"You could fold him up, shoot him, drown him, then *hang* him!" I added, getting into the game.

Dennis laughed.

Hey, I made him laugh! I told myself.

I suddenly wondered if my hair was messed up. I brushed a hand through it.

"You could fold him up, shoot him, drown him, then—"

I stopped when I saw Mr. Northwood standing in the classroom doorway, staring hard at us.

Oh, no! I thought, feeling my heart leap to my throat.

How long has he been standing there?

Has he heard everything?

chapter
4

Mr. Northwood glared at Dennis, then at me.

I let out a choking sound. I was sure he had heard me. I could feel my face grow hot. I knew it must be bright red.

But then, without saying a word, Mr. Northwood turned and headed away from us down the hall.

I just stood there, watching his head and shoulders bob as he took his usual long strides. I didn't start breathing again until he disappeared around the corner.

"I have to be nice to him," I whispered to Dennis. "He's my next-door neighbor. On Fear Street."

Dennis's mouth dropped open. "Huh? You live next door to Northwood?"

I nodded. "Do you believe it? I see him all the time. He's always messing around in the backyard, even in winter. It's like . . . it's like having a spy from school

21

next door. I always have the feeling he's checking up on me. I mean, I know he isn't. But still—"

I realized I was running on a bit at the mouth. I guess I was just so relieved that Mr. Northwood hadn't heard my diabolical plans to bump him off.

And I liked being able to confide in Dennis.

I'm usually really shy around boys. The old self-confidence problem. You know. But I suddenly had this feeling that I could talk to Dennis, that he and I were on the same wavelength.

"Northwood's neighbor. Weird," Dennis muttered, zipping his maroon and gray school jacket. "Weird." He slammed his locker shut and swung his backpack onto his shoulder.

"Weird enough living on Fear Street," I muttered.

Dennis snickered. "You believe all those stories? About ghosts and scary creatures on Fear Street?"

"Mr. Northwood is the scariest creature I've seen there!" I joked.

We both laughed.

We were walking side by side toward the parking lot exit. Our shoulders bumped a couple of times.

I was feeling super-charged. Really excited.

Dennis is just a great guy, I thought. So great-looking with that black hair over his broad forehead, and those eyes that could burn right into you like green fire.

I have to admit, it felt really great walking down the hall with one of the most popular guys at Shadyside High. I suddenly wished the school weren't empty. I wanted the halls to be crowded with kids so that everyone could see that Dennis and I were together.

We stepped out of the building into the dark gray afternoon. The air was heavy and wet.

"Looks like snow," Dennis commented, his eyes on the low clouds. "I'm glad Coach called off practice today." He headed along the walk to the student parking lot, and I followed.

Maybe he'd like to go get a Coke with me, I thought. We could just walk to The Corner. The Corner is a small coffee shop a couple of blocks from school, where Shadyside kids hang out.

A picture flashed into my mind: Dennis and me, sitting across from each other in a booth in The Corner, holding hands over the table, staring dreamily into each other's eyes.

What a picture.

I took a deep breath and worked up my courage to ask him if he wanted to get a Coke. "Uh . . . Dennis—?"

I stopped when I saw where Dennis was headed.

Right to the little red Miata stopped with its engine running at the end of the walk.

Caitlin's red Miata.

I could see her behind the wheel. She smiled and waved at Dennis as we approached.

Dennis turned to me at the end of the walk. "Sorry," he said. "I'd offer you a lift, but it's only a two-seater." He shrugged, then crossed to the passenger side to get in.

"That's okay, Dennis," I told him with a devilish smile. "I'll make room."

I pulled open the driver's door and grabbed Caitlin's arm with both hands. "Get out," I ordered.

"Huh?" Caitlin's dark eyes went wide in shock. "What?"

"Get out!" I cried.

I gripped her arm tight with one hand. Then I raised my other hand to her dark brown hair.

She screamed as I started to tug.

But I was too strong for her.

I jerked her out of the car, knocked her to the ground, and gave her a hard kick that sent her sprawling.

Then I slid behind the wheel, slammed the door, and drove the car away with Dennis beside me.

I glanced over at him to check out his reaction.

He was staring back at me with amazement and admiration.

chapter

5

After that Dennis realized that he and I belonged together. He dumped Caitlin, and we lived happily ever after.

Do you believe that?

No way.

Of course I didn't really pull Caitlin from the car.

Of course that wild little scene was all in my skinny little head.

What *really* happened was that I stood and watched as Dennis climbed into the car. Behind the wheel Caitlin stared right through me, as if I weren't even there.

Then she drove away with Dennis. Dennis didn't even look back.

And I was left standing there, my imagination playing out all kinds of evil scenes.

Why do I have such violent fantasies?

Why am I always picturing myself socking people in

the jaw, pushing people down stairs or off cliffs, tearing people's heads off and watching the blood gush up from their necks?

Why do I always imagine myself doing the most horrible, unspeakable things?

I guess it's because in real life I'm such a total mouse.

A week later there was an empty seat in history class. Dennis had gone to the Bahamas with his family.

Poor Dennis, I thought bitterly. He's missing the midterm exam tomorrow—and today he's missing a fascinating lecture on the separation of powers.

I was sitting in the back row, next to Melody Dawson. She held a pocket mirror in one hand and was brushing her perfect blond hair.

I had sat next to Melody all year and she had barely said two words to me. Every afternoon she would sit down, arrange her notebook on the desk, then brush her hair.

What a snob! Melody was always spotless and perfect. She wore French designer jeans that had been dry-cleaned. They had a perfect crease down the front. And almost all of her T-shirts and sweaters had the little Ralph Lauren polo pony on them.

Once I saw her changing into white sweat socks for gym—and *they* had polo ponies on them! Designer sweat socks! Do you believe it?

Melody has these perfect little lips and a perfect little upturned nose and perfect, creamy white skin.

The boys all think she's hot stuff. I just think she's a stuck-up snob.

Anyway, we were sitting in the back row on another dreary gray afternoon. I was thinking about Dennis. He was probably on a beach in the sun, swimming in sparkling blue water.

At the front of the room Mr. Northwood clicked on his little tape recorder and set it on the corner of his desk. "Do you know why I record our classes?" he asked. "I listen to them again later, at home."

He cleared his throat, his big Adam's apple bobbing under his gray turtleneck. "The tapes help me remember what we talked about," he continued in his thin, high voice. "I tape myself at home too. It can be very instructional."

Melody looked up from her mirror. "Why doesn't he get a life?" she said in a low voice.

Several kids snickered.

Mr. Northwood turned to Melody. "I heard that, Miss Dawson."

Melody stared back defiantly at him.

I would have turned bright red and shrunk back in my seat. I would have been totally mortified.

But Melody just glared back at him, almost challenging him.

"Melody, I'd like you to come see me after school," Mr. Northwood said sternly, scratching a craggy cheek. "You and I need to have a little talk."

"I can't," Melody replied coldly.

Mr. Northwood turned his watery blue eyes on her. "What did you say?"

"I can't," Melody repeated. "I have a tennis lesson."

The teacher tapped his long, bony fingers on the desktop. "I'm afraid you'll be late for your tennis lesson today," he said quietly.

"I'm afraid I won't!" I heard Melody mutter to herself.

Sure enough, as soon as class ended, Melody jumped up and ran out the door, hurrying to her tennis lesson.

Wow, I thought. That really takes nerve.

If Mr. Northwood had told *me* to stay after school, I'd obediently stay, no matter what I was missing. I'd be too afraid not to show up.

But Melody ran out without a second thought.

I didn't like Melody. I'd never liked her, actually. But I found myself wishing I had the nerve that she had.

I stood up and started gathering my books. Some kids were heading out the door to their lockers. I saw Zack Hamilton and Caitlin talking by the chalkboard.

Then I caught the angry expression on Mr. Northwood's face. "I don't care how many banks her father runs," he was fuming. "She's just like everybody else in my class!"

I saw Zack and Caitlin both laugh.

Mr. Northwood spun around to face them. "What are you two giggling about?" he demanded angrily. "Perhaps you'd like to stay an extra hour and discuss it with me!"

* * *

After dinner that night—a peanut butter sandwich and a small bag of potato chips—I was sitting cross-legged on the floor of my room, leaning against the bed, talking to Margaret on the phone.

My homework was spread out on my desk. But I just didn't feel like dealing with it.

I was feeling a little weird, a little jumpy. Sometimes living in an old house on Fear Street creeps me out when I'm all alone at night.

Outside the bedroom window, a light snow was falling. The wind gusted and swirled, making the old window rattle. Every once in a while, I could feel a cold burst of air on the back of my neck.

"I keep thinking about Dennis Arthur," I told Margaret. "You know. Down in the Bahamas, swimming and snorkeling and everything while we freeze."

"Yeah," Margaret replied, sighing. "Let's face it, Johanna. We have boring lives. I mean, the most exciting thing that happens to me is when somebody leaves a whole dollar tip at the restaurant."

"I should be working on my report," I murmured, yawning.

"Wow. Mr. Northwood is sure losing it these days," Margaret remarked. "I mean, he's been on everybody's case."

"Not everybody's," I corrected her.

"What do you mean?" Margaret asked.

"Well, haven't you noticed how he picks only on Dennis and his friends? You know. The rich kids. Caitlin and Melody—the group that was at the 7-Eleven that night last week."

Margaret was silent for a moment. I guess she was thinking about what I said. "Well," she piped up finally, "if he's picking only on the rich kids, I guess you and I have got it made!"

I snickered. "Yeah. I guess we're going to ace the course."

"Why do you think Northwood is on their case?" Margaret demanded.

I started to reply but stopped.

I heard the slam of a car door. Then I heard a crash downstairs.

Broken glass? A broken window?

"Margaret—I've got to go!" I cried. "I—I think someone is trying to break in!"

chapter
6

I felt a cold stab of dread as I jumped to my feet and ran to my bedroom window. The crash sounded as if it had come from the front of the house.

I stared down at the front yard. There were no streetlights on my block on Fear Street. But our porch light was on, sending a wash of pale yellow light over the small square of front lawn.

The snow had stopped. It had left small patches of white on the dark grass.

I pressed my forehead against the cold windowpane and stared down. No one on the front stoop or near the front of the house. No one in the front yard.

Then I saw dark shadows moving. At the bottom of Mr. Northwood's driveway. I saw a car parked at the curb. I saw three or four kids huddled behind Mr. Northwood's old Chevy Caprice.

I recognized Zack. Then I recognized Melody and Caitlin. Then I saw Lanny's blond hair. Yes. There were four of them, ducking low behind my neighbor's car.

What's going on? I wondered. What are they going to do?

I had a sudden picture of them setting Mr. Northwood's house on fire, then speeding away.

But that was too much. They wouldn't do that.

But what *were* they planning to do?

Impulsively I grabbed a big bulky sweater from my closet shelf and pulled it over my head as I hurried downstairs. Then, my breath trailing up in front of me, I ran down to the bottom of Mr. Northwood's driveway to greet them.

"Whoa!" Zack exclaimed in a low voice. "Johanna? What are *you* doing here?"

All four of them stared at me as if I were from Mars or something.

"I live here," I said, ducking behind Mr. Northwood's car beside Melody. I pointed to my house. I had left the front door wide open. It was going to get freezing cold in there, I realized. But I didn't want to run back and close the door.

"You live next door to Northwood?" Melody demanded. Those were the most words she had ever spoken to me.

"Yeah." I nodded. "Lucky, huh?"

"This whole street gives me the creeps," Caitlin complained.

Zack had a wool ski cap on his head. He pulled it down lower until it nearly covered his blue sunglasses. "Northwood belongs on Fear Street," he muttered. "With all the other ghouls."

I suppose I should have been insulted. But I was too excited to protest.

I admit it. I was really eager to see why these four kids had driven over from North Hills to pay a late-night visit on our beloved history teacher.

I had a feeling they hadn't come to deliver flowers.

"Hurry up," Melody urged them, slapping her leather gloves together. "It's cold and it's late. And you guys were making enough noise to wake up everyone in the cemetery." She motioned toward the Fear Street cemetery, which was about a block and a half down the street.

"His lights are out," Lanny whispered, peering up at the two-story brick house bathed in darkness. "He's asleep."

"I'd like to *punch* his lights out!" Zack muttered.

"What are you going to do?" I asked.

Lanny raised a finger to his lips. "You didn't see us here, Johanna," he said solemnly.

Zack turned to me. He looked kind of scary in the dark sunglasses and the ski cap pulled so low on his face. "You've got to swear you won't tell Northwood."

"Okay, okay," I told them impatiently. "I'm not a snitch, you know."

"Well, he *is* your neighbor," Melody said snootily. "You might want to get a few Brownie points by turning us in."

"No way," I insisted, stung by her cold accusation.

I was feeling excited and a little frightened at the same time. And I guess I wanted to be accepted by them, to sort of be considered part of their group.

So Melody's remark stung me extra hard.

She really let me know that she didn't trust me—and didn't think of me as a friend.

I wondered if the other three kids felt the same way.

They probably do, I thought miserably. Maybe I should just go back to the house and let them pull their stupid prank, whatever it is.

"I'm too cold," Caitlin said, shivering, her arms wrapped around herself. "I'm getting back in the car." She started across the street. In the dim light, I saw that the car was a dark-colored Mercedes.

"Chicken!" Zack called after her.

"Shhhhh!" Melody gave him a playful shove.

Zack turned to Lanny. "Go ahead. I dare you," he whispered to him.

"You dare me? I dare you!" Lanny shot back.

"I dared you first," Zack replied. "Come on, man. You know the rule. A dare's a dare. You've got to follow through. That's the rule."

"Okay, okay," Lanny said. He edged his way to the back of Mr. Northwood's car. I spotted a brown paper bag in his gloved hand. It was the size of a lunch bag.

"What's in it?" I whispered to Zack.

"Sand," he replied, his eyes on Lanny.

Ducking low behind the car, we all watched Lanny as he opened the flap over the gas tank and twisted off the cap. Then he emptied the bag of sand into Mr. Northwood's gas tank.

Zack and Melody laughed gleefully. Lanny crinkled the bag into a ball and tossed it onto the grass.

"Is that it?" Melody whispered. "Can we go now?"

"Wait," Zack said. Something gleamed in his hand.

It took me a few seconds to realize it was a knife blade.

"I never go anywhere without my Swiss Army knife," he whispered. He winked at me.

The knife made me a little scared. What was he going to cut?

"I think Mr. Northwood should have his car customized," Zack said, grinning under the wool cap. "You know. Autographed." He slid the blade against the back fender of the old Caprice.

"Whose name are you going to put?" Lanny demanded.

"Why not put *all* of our names?" Melody asked sarcastically. "Then Northwood will know who to give A's to this term."

Zack turned angrily to Melody. "I'm not stupid, you know!"

"So? Whose name?" Lanny demanded.

"Mr. Northwood's favorite guy," Zack said, grinning. "You dare me?"

"I dare you," Lanny replied.

Zack leaned over the car and began to scratch thick block letters into the paint of the back fender.

Feeling a mixture of fear and excitement, I moved forward to see what name he was writing.

D-E-N-N—

He had started to scratch in the *I* when Mr. Northwood's porch light flashed on.

"Oh!" Melody let out a frightened cry. She turned and ran to the car, her arms outstretched as if she wanted to take off and fly away.

Zack and Lanny were right behind her.

"Go! Go! Go!" Lanny was crying.

I watched the two boys dive into the backseat as Melody slid behind the wheel. The back door of the Mercedes was still open as she pulled the car from the curb and roared away.

Totally panicked, I was still standing behind Mr. Northwood's car. My heart was beating so hard, I thought my chest was going to explode.

I've got to get away from here! I realized.

I was halfway across my front yard, my sneakers slipping on the wet, frozen grass, when Mr. Northwood burst onto his front stoop.

"Johanna—what are you doing?" he shouted.

chapter

7

I froze in the middle of the front yard like a deer caught in car headlights.

"Johanna, what's going on?" Mr. Northwood demanded.

He stepped quickly off his front stoop and hurried to the driveway. He was wearing a gray turtleneck over baggy dark corduroys. His gray-white hair was standing nearly straight up on his head.

I glanced up at my open front door. Why hadn't I run when the others ran? The sound of the Mercedes roaring away lingered in my ears.

Why hadn't I run?

Mr. Northwood walked up to me, taking long, hurried strides, his breath steaming up in front of him. "Johanna?"

"I . . . uh . . ." I'm not a good liar. And I'm not the fastest-thinking person in the world. But I knew I had to come up with *something*.

"I . . . heard noises," I stammered, trying to sound calm and sincere. "Voices. I thought someone was trying to break in or something. So I came outside to . . . see who it was."

Pretty lame, I thought.

I stared hard into his eyes, trying to see if he believed me.

"I saw who it was," Mr. Northwood replied, frowning as he stared back at me.

My mouth formed a silent *O*. I could feel my face getting hot.

A strong gust of cold wind swirled over me. I could feel the cold even through my bulky sweater. Somewhere down the block I heard the clatter of a metal trash can being blown over.

"Since when do you hang around with *that* group, Johanna?" Mr. Northwood asked sternly. He lowered his face close to mine, so close I could smell onions on his breath.

"I—I don't," I replied, avoiding his harsh stare. "I just heard voices, that's all. I came out and then . . . I tried to get them to leave."

Does he believe *any* of this? I wondered.

I was so angry at myself for not being a better liar!

Mr. Northwood turned away from me without saying another word. Stooping his head, his hands shoved into his pants pockets, he made his way down the driveway to his car.

I crossed my fingers behind my back, hoping it was too dark for him to see the letters Lanny had scratched onto the back fender.

But I saw him lean close and run his fingers over the fender. His expression didn't change. But he stood there for a long while.

Then he spoke in a low voice, so low I could barely hear him over the gusting wind. "I'm calling the police," he said.

chapter

8

My heart pounding, I ran back to my house and slammed the door shut behind me. I was shaking all over, partly from the cold and partly from Mr. Northwood's threat.

I leaned against the banister and waited for my breathing to return to normal. I rubbed my arms, trying unsuccessfully to chase the chill away.

Were the police going to be knocking on my door in a few minutes?

Was I going to be arrested for messing up Mr. Northwood's old Chevy?

My mom will have a stroke! I told myself.

Mom wasn't around much because she was working so hard. But these days, when she *was* home she was acting very strict—I guess to make up for not being home.

I'll be grounded for life! I moaned to myself.

Mom will never trust me again.

And I didn't even *do* anything! I just watched them!

I paced back and forth in the living room for a while, listening for a police siren or sounds of an approaching car. I kept staring out the living room window. Then, seeing nothing but darkness, I'd go back to pacing, my hands shoved into my jeans pockets.

When car headlights rolled up over the living room wallpaper, I knew it was the police.

But it was only Mom, finally home from work.

She slumped in and dropped her bag on the floor with a weary sigh. "What's wrong with *you?*" she asked, eyeing me suspiciously.

I guess I wasn't doing a very good job of keeping my worries off my face. "Nothing," I replied quickly. "Just tired, I guess."

"Tell me about it," Mom replied, rolling her eyes.

The police never did show up.

I went to bed thinking that maybe Mr. Northwood had decided not to do anything after all.

But the next afternoon, there were four empty seats in his class. They had belonged to Lanny, Zack, Caitlin, and Melody.

All through Mr. Northwood's lecture, I kept staring at the empty seats.

When the bell rang, Mr. Northwood clicked off his little tape recorder and dismissed the class. As I stood up, I saw him motioning for me to come to his desk.

What does he want? I wondered. I studied his face, but I couldn't read his expression.

I took a deep breath and made my way to the front of the room.

"You're probably wondering where they are," Mr. Northwood said, gesturing to where the four kids usually sat. "Or has word traveled around school already?"

"I haven't heard anything," I replied nervously.

He leaned forward, spreading both of his long hands out on the desktop. "I had your four friends suspended from school," he said in a low voice just above a whisper.

"They're not really my friends," I insisted.

It was the truth, after all.

His expression remained a blank. The overhead lights made the deep crags that ran down his cheeks look like dark cuts.

Is he going to suspend me too? I wondered.

"The police didn't take it seriously," Mr. Northwood revealed, shaking his head, his blue eyes still locked on mine. "They came two hours later. They said it was just a prank."

He coughed, then cleared his throat. "It may have been a prank, but it was a *malicious* prank," the teacher continued, leaning over his desk. "I couldn't let it go unpunished. So I spoke to Mr. Hernandez. He suspended them this morning."

Is he going to have the principal suspend me too? I wondered, staring back at him. *Is* he?

Why is he taking so long?

What does he expect me to say?

He swallowed hard. His big Adam's apple bobbed up and down under his green turtleneck. He lifted his hands from the desk and raised himself to his full height.

"I believed your story last night," he said finally. "I know you don't run with that crowd. You're a nice girl. A good student."

"Thank you," I muttered awkwardly.

"I believed you, Johanna," Mr. Northwood repeated, licking his colorless lips. "But I'm going to be keeping an eye on you."

I picked up my books and hurried out of the classroom. As I made my way through the crowded hall to my locker, I got madder and madder.

"I'm going to be keeping an eye on you." His thin, reedy voice lingered in my ears.

Who does he think he is? I asked myself angrily. Just who does he think he is?

That night I was studying up in my room, struggling with a complicated chemistry equation until it became a blur of letters and numbers.

When the phone rang, I grabbed it before the first ring ended, happy for the interruption. I figured it was Margaret, calling to discuss the same problem—but it wasn't.

"Hello, Johanna?" a boy's voice said.

"Yes. Who's this?" I didn't recognize the voice. I didn't think it was anyone I'd ever talked to on the phone before.

"It's Dennis. Dennis Arthur."

I nearly gasped into the phone. I was so startled. Dennis was calling *me?*

"Hi, Dennis," I managed to choke out. "You're back from the Bahamas?"

"Yeah. This morning," he replied. And then he lowered his voice to just above a whisper. "Hey, Johanna," he murmured, "are you ready to kill Mr. Northwood?"

chapter

9

I laughed. "You're joking, right?"

I heard Dennis snicker at the other end of the line. "Yeah. I guess," he replied. "Wishful thinking."

There was an awkward silence.

"It's just that you had such good ideas when I talked to you that time," Dennis said.

"I have a lot of good ideas," I told him, trying to sound mysterious.

Why is he calling me? I wondered.

He just got back from vacation this morning. Why is he calling me tonight?

"How were the Bahamas?" I asked, trying to sound casual.

"Great," Dennis replied. "We had great weather. Only one rainy day. The beach was great for running."

"You're so lucky!" I exclaimed.

"I ran for miles on the beach. And I did a lot of

snorkeling with my dad," Dennis continued. "The reef was really outstanding. Do you snorkel?"

"Uh . . . no," I replied. It isn't easy to snorkel in your bathtub! I thought bitterly.

"On the last day I was snorkeling off by myself, and I accidentally brushed against some fire coral," Dennis continued. "Man, did that burn! I've got a huge red spot on my leg."

"Too bad," I murmured, trying to sound sympathetic.

On our last vacation, Mom and I went to visit her sister in Cleveland.

Listening to Dennis go on about the beach and how warm the ocean down there was, I found myself feeling more and more jealous. And I was practically bursting to find out the real reason for his call.

Finally he got around to it. "Are you busy Friday night?" he asked. He didn't give me time to answer. "I've been thinking about you. I mean, on vacation. There's a party Friday. At Melody's. Just a few kids. I thought maybe . . ."

I couldn't believe it! Dennis Arthur was asking me out!

The best-looking, most popular guy at Shadyside High was asking me to a party in North Hills.

I wanted to say *yes, yes, yes.*

But instead, I blurted out: "What about Caitlin?"

I don't really know why I asked it. It sort of slipped out automatically. I wanted to bite my tongue and take the words back. But of course it was too late.

"Caitlin and I go out with other people sometimes," Dennis replied with just a moment of hesitation.

"Really?" Again the word slipped out of my mouth. My brain was all messed up. I guess this was just too big a surprise. "I mean . . . will Caitlin be at the party?"

"No. She has to visit her cousin in Waynesbridge," Dennis replied. "Don't worry about Caitlin," he added. "It's no problem. Really. It's just a little party. We all usually get together at someone's house on Friday night. You want to go?"

"Yes. Great!" I said, finally getting my brain and my mouth to work together. "That'll be great, Dennis."

"Good," he said. "I'll be back at school tomorrow."

"You didn't miss much," I told him.

"Did you hear about Zack and the others?" he asked. "You know. Caitlin, Melody, and Lanny?"

"Yeah. I know all about it," I told him. "I was there the night they—"

"Yeah. I heard," he interrupted. "You live right next door, right? Well, did you hear they all got back in?"

"Huh?" I wasn't sure I understood. "You mean they're not suspended?"

"No way," Dennis replied. "Their parents went in to see Hernandez this afternoon. They really got on Hernandez's case. When they finished with him, he was shaking like a leaf. At least, that's what Melody's mom told my mom."

"Wow," I murmured. "Wow."

"Hernandez said they could all come back to school tomorrow morning," Dennis said, chuckling. "And he apologized for kicking them out in the first place."

"Wow," I repeated. I didn't know what else to say. I was stunned.

"I guess Northwood loses big," Dennis continued gleefully.

"I guess," I agreed.

Being rich really *is* different, I thought with some bitterness.

The parents of those four kids marched into school, and the principal backed down immediately. He even apologized!

If my mom went to school to complain, Mr. Hernandez wouldn't apologize to her, I knew. He wouldn't be afraid of her—because we're poor and we don't live in a big house in North Hills.

"See you tomorrow," Dennis said.

"See you tomorrow," I repeated. "And thanks."

I hung up. I had a smile on my face. I could see it in my dresser mirror.

Maybe this is the start of something great, I thought.

Maybe my life is going to start changing now.

Maybe I'm going to start hanging out with a whole new group of kids.

I'd do *anything* to be part of Dennis's group, I realized.

Anything!

Dennis was at his locker when I arrived at school the next morning. I dropped my backpack to the floor and started to work the combination on my locker door.

Dennis smiled at me. His green eyes seemed to light

up. He hadn't brushed his black hair, but it looked great anyway, all disheveled.

He is *so handsome!* I thought.

We said hi to each other. My stomach suddenly felt very feathery.

He walked over to me.

He's at least a foot taller than me, I realized.

I saw a white blur and then realized he was holding something up in front of him. "This is for you," he said shyly. "From the Bahamas."

I focused on it. A big, shiny pink and white conch shell.

"It's great!" I cried, reaching for it.

My mind was whirring. Dennis had actually brought *me* a present!

"Careful. It's kind of pointy there," he said.

I started to take it from him. It felt cold, from being outside.

The guy at the next locker accidentally bumped me, and I nearly dropped it. "It's great," I told Dennis. "Thanks."

"I was walking on the beach—" he started to say. But he stopped as Caitlin appeared beside him.

Caitlin was wearing a very tight-fitting white sweater. It looked like it might be cashmere. She had it pulled down over straight-legged black denim jeans. She had long, jangly silver earrings in her ears. Her short brown hair was swept straight back.

The smile on her face quickly vanished as her eyes caught the conch shell between my hands. "Hey!" Caitlin cried angrily.

"Hi," Dennis greeted her uncertainly. "I was looking for you."

Caitlin ignored him. She glared at me, then lowered her eyes again to the big shell. "Isn't that the shell you said you brought back for *me?*" she demanded of Dennis.

Dennis's mouth dropped open. "Whoa!" he exclaimed. His cheeks turned bright red. "I didn't—"

"What's going on here, Dennis?" Caitlin demanded angrily.

"Huh? What do you mean?" Dennis replied weakly.

"What's going on?" Caitlin repeated, staring at the conch shell. "I mean, why are you and Johanna—"

"Nothing!" Dennis insisted.

"Well, then . . ." Caitlin turned to me. "Give me my shell."

She reached out both hands for it, but I backed away, pulling the shell out of her reach.

"It's my shell, Johanna," Caitlin said through clenched teeth. "Dennis brought it for me. So let me have it."

I glanced at Dennis, then back at Caitlin.

Dennis was still blushing, as red as a tomato. He avoided my eyes. Caitlin was so angry, I could practically see smoke shooting out her ears.

This isn't right, I thought. This really isn't right.

"You want the shell, Caitlin?" I asked in a tight, shaky voice.

"Yes. Give me the shell. It's mine!" Caitlin insisted.

"Okay," I said. "Here."

And I smashed the shell as hard as I could into Caitlin's face.

I heard her teeth crack.

Bright red blood spurted from her mouth.

The sharp shell cut a flap in her cheek, and blood rolled down the side of her face.

The shell dropped to the floor and shattered.

Caitlin staggered back against the lockers and raised her hand to her bleeding cheek.

She tried to say something. But she choked on the spurting blood.

I raised my eyes to Dennis. He had a pleased smile across his handsome face.

chapter
10

Of course, I imagined the part about smashing Caitlin with the conch shell.

Just another one of my sick, violent fantasies.

It's amazing the things I imagine. I guess it's just my way of dealing with the world. You know. Getting things out of my system.

What *really* happened was that Caitlin didn't notice me or the conch shell.

She appeared beside Dennis, wrapped her hand in his, and they strolled off together. Dennis turned his head and mouthed a silent "Bye" in my direction. Then he walked off hand in hand with Caitlin to homeroom.

Leaving me there to dream up my nasty little scene of broken teeth and spurting blood.

After a few moments, the bell rang, stirring me from my troubling thoughts. I slid the shell onto the top shelf of my locker and hurried down the rapidly emptying hall.

At lunch Margaret and I were sitting across from each other in the cafeteria, scooping up blueberry yogurt from little containers. Margaret was telling me a funny story about her twin cousins, when she suddenly stopped.

She was facing the double doors to the lunch room, and I saw she was staring over my shoulder toward them. "What's up?" I asked, not bothering to turn around.

"Oh, nothing," she replied, still staring. "Did you say Dennis asked you out for Friday?"

"Yeah," I replied. "Why?"

I couldn't resist any longer. I turned all the way around to see what Margaret found so interesting behind me.

It didn't take long to figure out what my friend was gawking at.

Outside the open doors and across the hall, I could see Dennis and Caitlin. He had his back to the lunch room, but I instantly knew it was him. He had Caitlin pressed against the wall, and he was kissing her.

Practically in front of the entire lunch room!

I wheeled back around in my chair, feeling really upset. I glanced across the table to see Margaret staring at me, tugging at a strand of her carrot-colored hair.

"Don't stare at me," I grumbled.

"You sure he called you?" she asked quietly. "You sure it was *the* Dennis Arthur?"

"Ha-ha," I said bitterly. I kept my eyes on Margaret. "Are they still kissing back there?"

Margaret nodded. "Maybe their braces got locked together," she suggested.

"They don't wear braces," I muttered unhappily.

"I wonder why he asked you out," Margaret said thoughtfully.

"You have a yogurt mustache," I told her.

But secretly I wondered too.

After our last period history class, Dennis had another argument with Mr. Northwood. Again I lingered in the back of the room, eavesdropping and wishing Mr. Northwood would give Dennis a break.

"You've *got* to give me a makeup test!" Dennis was pleading. His face was bright red, and he was sweating even though the windows were open and it was cold in the room.

"I don't *have* to do anything except pay taxes and die," Mr. Northwood replied quietly, staring back at Dennis with a strange, tight-lipped smile on his craggy face.

Mr. Northwood is *enjoying* making Dennis beg and squirm, I suddenly realized.

It must be the feeling of power, I guessed. Mr. Northwood really has a cruel streak.

"You're going to ruin my life!" Dennis was screaming. He had both hands on the front of the teacher's desk and was leaning over so that he and Mr. Northwood were practically face-to-face.

"I don't want to ruin your life. I want to teach you a little about fairness," Mr. Northwood replied, still talking softly and deliberately. "You and I have already discussed this, Dennis."

"But if I get a failing grade, I won't be eligible for the all-state team. And then there goes the Olympic tryouts!" Dennis cried, his voice high-pitched and shrill.

"Let us hope you don't get a failing grade," Mr. Northwood said coldly. He began shuffling through a notebook.

Dennis let out a frustrated groan. "You really won't give me a makeup test?"

Mr. Northwood shook his head. "I have to be fair to everyone."

"But you're being unfair to *me!*" Dennis cried, starting to lose his temper.

"I don't think so," the teacher replied, stone-faced, shuffling through the notebook.

"Can I do a project or something for extra credit?" Dennis demanded.

Mr. Northwood shook his head. "I appreciate your situation," he said. "But I really cannot bend the rules for one student."

Dennis raised both hands above his head in a gesture of futility. Then, with a loud sigh, he spun away from the teacher's desk. Taking long, angry strides, he headed toward the door.

I stepped away from the wall, eager to talk to Dennis, to try to say something encouraging him.

I thought he was coming to me.

"Dennis—" I started to say.

I uttered a little cry of surprise as he walked right past me.

He didn't say a word to me. He just kept walking.

And then I saw Caitlin. She was waiting for him outside the door.

He walked up to her. She leaned close to him, whispered something to him, and then they disappeared from view.

What is going on here? I asked myself unhappily.

I stared at the empty doorway.

Is Dennis interested in me or not? I wondered.

If he's so hung up on Caitlin, why did he ask me out for Friday night?

Friday night Dennis was supposed to pick me up at eight o'clock. I must have glanced at the clock on my dresser top a thousand times.

I was so nervous, my hands were as cold and clammy as two wet fish. I was sure he wouldn't show.

All sorts of troubling thoughts flashed through my mind. Maybe his call was just a cruel joke, I thought. Maybe it was one of their dares. They were always daring each other to do weird things. Lanny or Zack probably dared him to call me. Then Dennis and his pals had a good laugh at my expense.

Or maybe I imagined the whole thing. Maybe he never asked me out at all. Maybe it was all one of my fantasies.

I changed my sweater three times. I don't know why. They were all pretty much the same.

I'd found earrings at the mall that looked like little conch shells. I put them on, studied them in the mirror, took them off, then put them on again.

My clock read 8:03, but it was always a little fast.

I brushed my hair with rapid strokes. Maybe I should cut it short, I thought. Seeing the cleft in my chin made me frown at myself. Why couldn't I have a smooth chin like normal people?

I was still staring unhappily at myself in the mirror when the doorbell rang. I heard Mom's footsteps downstairs. I heard her pull open the door. I heard Dennis's voice.

He's really here! I thought. It isn't a joke.

I took one last look at myself in the mirror, then hurried downstairs to greet him.

Melody's house was big and very modern. The living room furniture was all chrome and soft white leather. The walls were covered with framed movie posters. Track lighting on the ceiling cast pale triangles of light over the room.

"How's it going?" Melody asked me as she led us into the room. She eyed my yellow sweater. I suddenly felt even more self-conscious. Maybe I should've worn the blue one.

"My parents are at the movies," Melody told Dennis. "The house is all ours!" She didn't seem at all surprised to see me with Dennis instead of Caitlin.

I saw eight or nine kids as Dennis and I followed Melody across the room. They were all from school, but I knew only a few of them. Most of them were seniors.

Lanny and Zack were standing in front of a TV in the corner, staring at a basketball game, taking long sips from cans of beer. A red-haired girl I didn't know kept asking them to turn down the sound so she could put on music, but they ignored her.

Two couples had squeezed onto the couch and were laughing loudly about something. The two boys slapped each other high-fives.

Two girls were at the table against the wall, helping themselves to sections of an enormous submarine sandwich. The girls both had long, frizzy blond hair that shimmered in the cones of light from overhead.

"You get anywhere with Northwood?" Melody asked Dennis. Before Dennis could reply, the doorbell rang, and Melody hurried to answer it.

"You know these kids?" Dennis asked, turning to me. He was wearing a denim vest over a blue workshirt and faded jeans torn at the knees.

"Some of them," I replied.

"Most of them live in North Hills," Dennis told me. He motioned to the red-haired girl who was entering the room with Melody. "You know her? That's Reva Dalby. Her family owns all those department stores."

"Hey, what's up?" Dennis called to Reva. The two of them talked for a short while about a tennis instructor they both had. I stood close to Dennis, but Reva didn't seem to notice I was there.

Dennis and I got Cokes. Then I followed him as he joined Lanny and Zack in front of the TV. He started teasing Lanny about the red jeans he was wearing. "I dare you to wear those to the dance at the club," Dennis said.

"Hey—no dares tonight," Lanny protested.

"Chicken," Dennis muttered.

Lanny pretended to get angry. They started laughing and playfully shoving each other, and Lanny spilled some of his beer on the white carpet.

"That's okay," Lanny said, making sure Melody wasn't watching. "Beer is good for the rug."

Several more kids arrived. They all seemed to know one another. Melody got her CD player going and drowned out the sound of the basketball game. I saw a couple making out on the stairway by the front door.

Since Dennis was busy kidding around with Lanny and Zack, I made my way to the table and took a section of the sub sandwich. I talked with some kids from my English class. "You're Margaret Rivers' friend," someone said to me. "She's very funny."

I wondered what Margaret was doing tonight. I wondered what I would tell her about this party, about my date with Dennis.

So far there wasn't much to tell. Dennis was pretty much ignoring me.

Around eleven o'clock, some kids left. The rest of us were sitting on the two couches or sprawled on the floor, eating tortilla chips and salsa and drinking Cokes.

Melody had turned the music off. A conversation started about school.

Dennis and I were sitting close together at an end of a couch. He was leaning forward, picking up handfuls of tortilla chips from the bowl on the glass coffee table. I was leaning back against the cushiony couch, not really part of the conversation.

Actually, I was wondering if Dennis liked me or

not. He hadn't been unfriendly. But he hadn't spent much time talking with me either.

The couch was jammed with kids. Dennis and I sat so close together, our legs were touching. He didn't seem to notice. Or was he just pretending not to notice?

All night I had been trying to relax and have a good time. But it was hard. This just wasn't my crowd. I didn't take private tennis lessons, so I couldn't gossip about the different tennis instructors. And I couldn't compare Jamaica to Bermuda or Aruba.

Everyone had been friendly to me. No one had acted at all snobby. But I could see that they were all better dressed than I was.

And Melody's house was so luxurious compared to my run-down old house on Fear Street. Even though I kept telling myself that it all didn't matter, I just couldn't relax and feel comfortable.

I wasn't really listening to the conversation. But when Dennis suddenly draped an arm around my shoulders, I instantly tuned back in.

And then Dennis totally surprised me by announcing to everyone, "Johanna and I are going to murder Mr. Northwood!" He turned to me, a big smile on his face. "Right?"

chapter

11

"*U*h . . . right," I reluctantly agreed.

"We're *doing* it!" Dennis proclaimed, squeezing my shoulder.

Everyone laughed and cheered.

What's going on here? I asked myself. Isn't Dennis taking this joke a little too far?

"I want to help!" someone exclaimed.

"Me too!"

"Let's *all* kill him!"

"Tonight!" someone added.

Everyone laughed.

"I dare you!" Lanny cried. "I really dare you!"

"Do it!" someone shouted.

Lanny turned to me. "How are you going to do it?" he demanded.

I formed a gun with my thumb and pointer finger and aimed it at Lanny.

Everyone laughed again.

Climbing to his feet, Zack pulled up his hair until it stood straight up on his head. Then he stooped his shoulders and did a pretty good impression of Mr. Northwood: "I don't like your smiles. You're all staying after school for the rest of the century. We're having a short quiz. Take out a sheet of paper and number from one to three thousand."

We were all in hysterics. Zack really was a riot. He sounded just like Mr. Northwood, and he kind of looked like him with his hair straight up like that.

"Did you hear what Northwood did to Carter Philips?" Lanny asked, shaking his head. "Northwood took five points off Carter's final exam because she forgot to put her name on top. The five points lowered Carter from a B to a C!"

Everyone groaned.

"He made me stay an hour after school on my birthday!" a girl on the other couch cried.

"What a jerk!" someone said.

"He really hates us all," Melody murmured.

"Not as much as we hate him," Lanny said.

"Don't worry," Dennis told them, grinning. "Johanna and I are going to take care of him. We've been making plans."

"When?" someone demanded. "Before the next unit test?"

Dennis smiled at me. His arm tightened around me. "It's a secret," he told them, his green eyes flashing excitely. "We don't want to spoil the surprise."

I laughed along with everyone else.

But I felt a sudden chill.

Was Dennis getting serious about this?

The idea of killing Mr. Northwood had started out as a joke.

It was still just a joke—right?

I was so surprised when Dennis kissed me.

When he drove me home, the car radio was on so loud we couldn't talk. He pulled up my driveway, then switched off the engine and the lights.

And he reached across the seat and pulled me close.

The kiss was awkward at first. I was just so startled.

But then I slid my hands behind his head, wrapping my fingers through his silky dark hair, holding his face against mine.

The kiss lasted a long time. When it ended, I was breathless.

He likes me, I thought.

I can tell. He really likes me.

Waiting for my breathing to return to normal, I glanced up at my house. It was entirely dark except for the light over the front stoop.

The bare branches of the two entwined maple trees in the center of the front yard shivered in the cold breeze. Fat brown leaves scrabbled like dark shadows over the frosted grass.

"I'm glad I asked you out," Dennis said softly.

"Me too," I murmured.

He reached out his arms for me again. This time I slid comfortably to him, and we kissed for a long time.

Thoughts about Caitlin forced their way into my mind as I wrapped my arms tighter around Dennis and kissed him. I shut my eyes and willed Caitlin away. Far away.

I opened my eyes when the kiss ended.

What was that tingling feeling on the back of my neck?

Still tasting Dennis's lips on mine, I had the sudden feeling that we were being watched.

I pulled away from him.

"Johanna—what is it?" Dennis whispered.

I gazed out the windshield, my eyes searching the darkness—and gasped in horror.

chapter

12

Mr. Northwood!

He was just standing there in his yard. Like a statue.

He had a large stick in one hand. A fallen tree branch. He was leaning on it like a cane.

Standing in deep shadows a few yards from the driveway. Leaning on the stick. Staring into the car.

Just standing and staring at us.

Dennis turned toward the windshield and followed my gaze. "Hey—" he cried. "What's *he* doing?"

"I—I don't know," I stammered. "He's watching us, I think."

Behind us a car rolled quietly down Fear Street. As its headlights played over the still form of Mr. Northwood, I caught the stern, disapproving expression set on his face.

"What a creep!" Dennis declared. "What a total creep."

"Let's just ignore him," I suggested, turning to Dennis with a devilish smile.

Dennis scowled in Mr. Northwood's direction. "No. I'd better go, Johanna."

"Want to come in for a while?" I suggested.

Dennis shook his head. His eyes were still on Mr. Northwood. "I'd better go. See you Monday, okay?"

"Okay." I pushed open the car door. A burst of cold air greeted me. Waving good-night to Dennis, I climbed out and ran to my front door.

Out of the corner of my eye, I caught Mr. Northwood still standing there, frozen like a snowman in his long gray overcoat.

Why is he standing there? I wondered angrily.

Is he really *spying* on me?

Dennis's headlights slid over me as he backed down the drive. I was so furious at Mr. Northwood, my hand shook as I tried to slide my key into the front door.

What right does he have to spy on me?

What business is it of his?

What is he doing out here?

Finally I got the key in the lock, twisted it, and pushed the door open.

The house was warm and smelled of the roast chicken we'd had for dinner. I was trembling all over as I tossed my coat over the banister.

Mr. Northwood spoiled my date, I thought bitterly.

Dennis and I were feeling so close to each other—and that creep Northwood spoiled it all.

My anger boiled up into a rage.

I realized my hands were balled into tight fists.

Without thinking, I made my way to the little green side table against the living room wall.

The living room was dark. I pulled open the drawer in the table. My hand fumbled around inside it until I found what I was looking for.

The pistol.

The pistol my dad had left us for protection when he moved out.

It felt sleek and cool in my hot, hot hand.

I wasn't thinking clearly. I was too furious to think clearly.

Why was he spying on me?

Why?

Without realizing it, without thinking about what I was doing, I made my way to the window. The pistol was gripped tightly in my hand.

Leaning against the glass, I peered out into the darkness.

There he was. Mr. Northwood hadn't moved. He was leaning on the tree branch, smoking a pipe. I could see the gray smoke swirl up against the purple sky.

Why did you spoil my date, Mr. Northwood?

What right do you have to spy on me and ruin my life?

Don't you know how much tonight meant to me?

I was trembling with anger. With a shaking hand I pulled up the window. The cold air felt good against my face.

My eyes on Mr. Northwood, I pulled back the hammer of the pistol, the way my dad had shown me.

Killing Mr. Northwood is so easy, I told myself.

67

So incredibly easy.

Leaning against the windowsill to steady myself, I raised the pistol.

I aimed it at Mr. Northwood.

Steady, steady.

I slid my finger over the trigger.

So incredibly easy. So easy to kill him.

I aimed for his chest.

And suddenly the living room lights flashed on.

"Johanna!" my mother exclaimed, bursting into the room. "What are you doing with that gun?"

Too late, Mom.

I pulled the trigger.

chapter

13

Of course the pistol wasn't loaded. The cartridge with the bullets was still in the drawer.

Lowering the pistol to my side, I turned to my mom. "I—I thought I heard a burglar," I lied.

"A burglar!" Mom cried, her eyes widening in alarm. "I'll call the police!"

"No. Wait," I told her. "There's no one there. I just heard the wind or something. You know how I get freaked at night sometimes."

"Close the window," my mom said, eyeing me suspiciously. "It's cold enough in this drafty old house."

Peering out into the dark front yard, I pushed the window down. To my surprise, Mr. Northwood had disappeared.

I guessed he had finally returned to his house.

I wish I could *really* make you disappear, I thought, still feeling shaky.

"You shouldn't take that gun out," Mom said, tightening the belt on her pink terrycloth robe. "I really don't want it in the house. It's just one more example of your father's poor judgment." She sighed.

"It isn't loaded," I said softly. I dropped it into the drawer and slid the drawer shut.

"How was your date?" Mom asked, her dark eyes boring into me, studying me.

"Great," I told her. "Really great."

As I hurried up to my room, I wondered if Dennis would ever ask me out again.

Melody cornered me in the girls' locker room in school Monday morning.

We had just played volleyball in gym. Melody's normally perfect hair was actually a little messed up. "I want to tell you something," she said, her pale blue eyes narrowed at me.

"We're going to be late," I told her. "The bell is going to ring."

"It won't take long," she replied, keeping her voice low. "You know, Caitlin found out about you and Dennis." She stared hard at me, watching my reaction.

I didn't react much. I let my mouth drop open in surprise, but I didn't say anything.

"I didn't tell her," Melody said, letting the towel she was holding drop to the bench between the lockers. "But she found out. There were so many kids at my house Friday night. I mean, she was bound to find out."

"So?" I asked, glancing up at the clock.

"So she's very upset," Melody continued. "I don't know what Dennis told you. But Caitlin can be very jealous. I just thought I should warn you. Caitlin doesn't want anyone else going out with Dennis."

"I think that's up to Dennis, isn't it?" I asked shrilly. I didn't mean to sound so intense, but I couldn't help it.

"Well, don't have a cow!" Melody exploded nastily. "I was just trying to give you a friendly warning."

The bell rang, startling us both. Applying lip gloss as she ran, Melody hurried away.

What's going on? I wondered.

I knew that Caitlin and Melody were pals. Did Caitlin send Melody to warn me? Did Dennis lie when he told me that he and Caitlin sometimes go out with other people? Was Melody just being vicious, just trying to stir up trouble?

The questions repeated in my head as I hurried to class. But no answers came to me.

After school I was making my way through the crowded halls to the library on the second floor. I had to get some material on cloning for a science project Margaret and I were working on together.

I passed Caitlin going the other way on the stairs. I was pretty sure she saw me, but she kept on talking to the girl beside her and stepped right by me.

At the top of the stairs, I turned toward the library. I stopped when I heard a familiar voice calling my name.

"Oh, hi, Dennis," I said, flashing him a warm smile. "What's up?"

He was wearing his maroon and gray Shadyside jacket over baggy faded jeans. He had a half-eaten granola bar in his hand. Smiling back at me, he offered me a bite.

I shook my head. "No, thanks."

He pulled a piece of thread off the shoulder of my blue sweater. "Want to study together tonight?" he asked. "I could come over after track practice."

He *does* like me! I thought happily.

Melody suddenly pushed her way into my mind. Again I saw her eyeing me sternly, warning me about Caitlin.

Dennis took a bite of the granola bar, waiting for my answer.

"That would be great!" I told him. I probably shouldn't have let myself sound so excited. I should have acted more casual about it. But I couldn't help it.

Sorry, Caitlin, I thought. I really like Dennis. And if Dennis really likes me, it's just too bad for you.

"Later," Dennis said, giving me a funny little two-finger salute.

"Later," I repeated happily.

By the time I got home, I was having second thoughts.

I mean, my house is so shabby and run-down. It's embarrassing.

Melody's house is like a palace compared to mine. It's five times as big, for one thing. And forget about chrome and white leather. Our living room is filled with a worn-out corduroy couch and two beat-up vinyl armchairs.

Pitiful. Really pitiful.

Gazing unhappily around the living room, I was tempted to call Dennis and make up some excuse why he couldn't come over. I wanted him to like me so much. And I was really afraid when he saw what my house looked like that he would decide I couldn't be part of his crowd.

Crazy thinking, I guess.

But Dennis had me a little unbalanced. I admit it.

I made myself a tuna fish sandwich for dinner and piled the plate high with potato chips. That's one great advantage of being as skinny as I am. You can eat as many potato chips as you like.

When the phone rang after my lonely dinner, I ran to answer it.

It's Dennis calling with an excuse for why he can't come over, I thought.

"Hello?" I swallowed hard, expecting to hear his voice.

"Hi, Johanna, it's me." Margaret. "What time should I come over?"

"Huh?" Margaret's question caught me by surprise.

"You said we'd work at your house tonight—remember?" Margaret said. "You know. On our science project?"

"Oh. Right." Dennis had me so crazed, I had totally forgotten about my plan to get together with Margaret.

"Uh . . . I can't do it tonight, Margaret. I . . . uh . . ."

I didn't want to tell her I was dumping her for Dennis. She and I really did have to work on the project. It was due on Friday.

"I think I'm getting the flu," I blurted out.

I'm such a bad liar. It was the first thing that popped into my head.

"You seemed fine in school today," Margaret insisted. I could tell she didn't quite believe me.

"I just started to feel sick after school," I told her, feeling really guilty. "I'm going to bed early. Maybe I'll be okay tomorrow. Want to get together tomorrow night?"

"Yeah, I guess," Margaret replied. "Feel better, okay?"

She hung up.

I stood there, thinking about Margaret, about what a good friend she was.

Why did I lie to her? I asked myself. Why didn't I just tell her that Dennis was coming over to study tonight?

Margaret would be *happy* for me.

No, she wouldn't, I decided. She'd be angry and hurt that I stood her up for Dennis. I did the right thing by telling a little white lie.

The doorbell rang. I hurried to answer it.

"Dennis—hi!" I called eagerly.

I pulled open the front door—and stared in amazement.

chapter
14

"*H*ey, how's it going?" Dennis grinned at me.

Four other faces peered in at me. Dennis had brought a whole group—Melody, Zack, Lanny, and even Caitlin!

They pushed past me into the house, all talking at once. I flashed Dennis a what's-going-on-here? look, but he didn't seem to notice.

After tossing their coats on a chair, they sprawled around the living room, talking and laughing, dropping their backpacks to the floor, pretty much ignoring me.

Melody stretched her legs over the arm of a brown vinyl armchair. She was wearing a long red sweater over black tights. Her blond hair was twisted up in a tight bun behind her head. "What are we doing here?" she asked Dennis. "Are we studying, or what?"

"We're partying," Zack said, grinning. He had

dropped his large Hulk body onto the floor. He was wearing his blue sunglasses, as usual. He turned to me. "Do you have anything to drink?"

"I think there are some Cokes in the fridge," I replied.

"I like your house," Lanny said, tapping a hand on the shabby corduroy couch. "It's real . . . comfortable."

"Is anyone else home?" Caitlin asked, glancing around. She stood very close to Dennis, who was sitting on the windowsill. She brushed something off the shoulder of his sweatshirt.

Caitlin had a navy blue baseball cap pulled down over her short brown hair. Her cheeks were red, from the cold outside, I guessed.

I told her my mom was at work. Then I went to see if there were enough Cokes for everyone.

Why didn't Dennis warn me? I wondered as I made my way to the kitchen. Why didn't he tell me he was bringing over all his friends?

I was disappointed that he hadn't come alone. But I was also happy to have them all in my house. I mean, maybe this meant they were accepting me into the group. Maybe this meant we were all going to be friends.

I bent down and started pulling cans of Coke out of the fridge. I could hear Caitlin laughing about something in the other room.

I felt a little uncomfortable having Caitlin there. Especially after what Melody had told me. But Caitlin didn't seem to be angry or anything. In fact, she seemed to be in a really good mood.

Did she really tell Melody to warn me to stay away from him? Did she even care?

It was all too confusing. I decided to just stay cool and try to enjoy my new friends.

"Hope you don't mind the crowd scene." Dennis suddenly appeared in the kitchen doorway. He smiled at me, a little-boy smile.

"No problem." I returned his smile. I had a sudden impulse to run over to him and throw my arms around him. He was just so great-looking.

Uh-oh, Johanna, I thought. Watch out. You're really falling for him. Watch out!

Dennis helped me carry in the Cokes. When we returned to the living room, the mood had changed.

Zack had climbed to his feet and was lumbering back and forth in front of the window. "Do you believe that jerk?" he was demanding. He scratched his curly red hair as he paced. "Do you believe him?"

"Who are you talking about?" Dennis asked him, sitting down on the floor beside Caitlin.

"Northwood, of course," Zack replied bitterly. "Didn't you hear about it, Dennis? I'm sure it was all over school."

"What was?" Dennis asked. He took a long swig from his Coke can, his green eyes locked on Zack.

"Northwood called Zack up after class. He caught him cheating on the quiz," Lanny said, an amused grin on his face.

"I *wasn't* cheating!" Zack screamed, glaring at Lanny.

"Then why were you leaning over Deena Martinson's shoulder?" Melody demanded.

"I was asking her what time it was," Zack replied. "I wasn't looking at her answers. I was asking for the time."

Melody and Lanny laughed scornfully. Caitlin rolled her eyes.

"We don't believe you," Dennis said softly, snickering.

Zack exploded, letting out a string of curses. I couldn't see his eyes behind the blue sunglasses. But I didn't need to see them to know he was really angry. He is so big and powerful-looking, I was afraid he might shove his fist through the window or smash all the lamps.

I had a momentary fantasy of Zack going on a rampage in my living room. I pictured Mom getting home, walking in, and finding nothing left but sawdust.

Which would be an improvement.

"It's no lie," Zack declared. "No lie. I wasn't cheating. But Northwood grabbed me and pulled me out of the room. He said he could have me suspended again, this time for good."

"Did you tell him you were asking for the time?" Dennis asked.

"Of course," Zack shot back bitterly. "But Northwood wouldn't listen. He wouldn't even let me talk!"

"He won't listen to any of us," Lanny broke in, his handsome features set in a hard frown beneath his blond hair. "And he won't give us a break. You know why? You know why Northwood is always on our case?"

"Because he's a jerk?" Zack answered.

"No. Because we're rich," Lanny said heatedly. "We're rich and he's poor. And that's why *we're* the ones he always picks on."

"Yeah, you're right," Melody murmured.

"He never gives us a break," Caitlin agreed.

Zack suddenly bent over and hoisted up his backpack. "That's okay," he muttered. "That's okay." He unzipped it and reached one of his beefy hands inside. After a few seconds of fumbling through the stuff in the backpack, he appeared to find what he was looking for.

When Zack turned back to the rest of us, his expression quickly changed. Beneath the round blue sunglasses, an evil smile crossed his face.

"Hey, man, what's in there?" Dennis demanded.

"I'm going to take care of him," Zack replied, his grin growing wider, his expression menacing. "I'm going to take care of Northwood—tonight."

chapter

15

Dennis and Lanny started to laugh. But something about Zack's expression made them cut it short.

I was standing behind the couch, my arms crossed tensely in front of me. Everyone stared at Zack.

He let his backpack drop to the floor at his feet. It took me a while to recognize what he gripped in his big, chunky hand.

A test tube.

Still grinning, Zack held it up so we all could see it.

"Wh-what *is* it?" I stammered.

"Zack's going to drink it and turn into a werewolf," Melody commented dryly.

The yellow liquid inside the test tube glistened in the light.

"It's nitroglycerin!" Lanny declared, jumping to his feet. "He's going to blow us all up!"

Zack let out an evil, mad-scientist laugh and held the slender glass tube above his head.

"Give us a break," Caitlin pleaded. "What *is* it, Zack?"

"Skunk juice," Zack revealed.

"Huh?" We all let out cries of surprise.

"It's skunk scent," Zack repeated, stepping toward us, stretching the test tube toward us. "Here. Want a sniff?" He reached to remove the cork cap.

"Yuck!"

"No way!"

"Get *out* of here!"

"Is it really skunk scent?" I asked, staring hard at the yellow liquid.

Zack nodded. "Yeah. My brother got it for me. From a science lab at the university."

"That's really gross," Caitlin murmured, making a face.

"Want a sip?" Zack held it out to her.

"Get away!" Caitlin screamed. She buried her face in Dennis's sweatshirt.

I felt a pang of jealousy. I wanted to be sitting where Caitlin was—next to Dennis.

But I didn't have time to think about that. Suddenly everyone was standing, following Zack to the front door.

"What are you going to do?" Caitlin demanded, pulling on her parka.

"He's going to drink it and then go breathe on Northwood," Dennis suggested.

Everyone laughed.

"Way to go, man!" Lanny slapped Zack hard on the back, nearly making him drop the test tube.

"Whoa!" I cried. I had a nightmare vision of my entire house smoldering with skunk scent.

"Come on, Zack, what's your plan? Where are we going?" Melody asked, turning at the front door and blocking the way. "I'm not going with you guys till I know what you're doing."

Zack grinned at her beneath his blue glasses. "Simple," he said, holding the test tube waist-high. "One of us will pour this stuff on Northwood's front stoop. That's all. My brother said it'll take months for the stink to go away."

"One of us?" Dennis demanded. "What do you mean, *one* of us?"

"Well, I got the skunk juice," Zack replied. "So someone else should drop it. Here, Dennis. I dare you."

He tried to hand the test tube to Dennis, but Dennis raised his hands and backed away. "No way, man!" he cried. "I'm in enough trouble with Northwood!"

"It's revenge, Dennis!" Zack insisted, holding out the glass tube. "Revenge! You *know* you want to do it. Come on. I'm daring you!"

"No way," Dennis repeated. He rested a hand on Caitlin's shoulder.

"It's your skunk juice. *You* pour it," Melody told Zack.

"I'm too big. Northwood will see me—" Zack started to say.

"I'll do it!" I exclaimed.

Don't ask me why I volunteered. The words just popped out of my mouth.

I think it had something to do with seeing Caitlin rest her hand on Dennis's shoulder. I think I really wanted to impress Dennis. I wanted to show everyone that I was one of them, one of the group. And I wanted to show Dennis that I was more fun than Caitlin.

I didn't think of those reasons until later. I didn't have any reasons in my head when I just blurted out that I'd do it.

"Way to go, Johanna!" Lanny cried.

Zack slipped the test tube into my hand. It felt warm from the tight grip he had had on it. "Johanna's a shrimp," Zack explained to the others. "She can sneak up there, do the job, and then sneak away without being seen."

"You're just a wimp," Dennis accused Zack.

Zack playfully shoved a big fist into Dennis's face. "Say that again. I'll mess you up, man."

Dennis made a disgusted face. "Hey, Zack, that skunk juice came off on your hand. Phew!"

"Huh?" Zack let out an unhappy cry and started furiously sniffing his hand.

Dennis laughed. "Gotcha!"

Zack pounded him hard in the shoulder.

"Hey, are we going to stand here all night? Let's go do it!" Lanny exclaimed.

We stepped out into a still, cold night. A bright half-moon hovered low over the bare trees. Nothing moved. Not a leaf stirred. It was eerily quiet.

I led the way to Mr. Northwood's house. I was glad

to see that the house was entirely dark. Maybe he isn't home, I thought. Or maybe he went to bed early.

We crossed my driveway and stopped at the side of Mr. Northwood's house. Two rather pitiful evergreen shrubs grew there, and we all ducked behind them.

"His car isn't in the driveway," Dennis whispered. "So he probably isn't home."

"It might be in his garage," I whispered back.

I realized I was gripping the test tube so tightly, I might smash it. I loosened my hold on it as I stared over at the dark front stoop.

Why am I doing this? I asked myself. Have I lost my mind totally?

I glanced at Dennis. He winked back at me encouragingly.

My heart skipped. Yes. Maybe I *have* lost my mind, I told myself.

Would I do *anything* for Dennis? I wondered.

There was no time to think about that. The others were all whispering, urging me on.

I took a deep breath and started jogging across the grass to Mr. Northwood's front stoop. I held the test tube carefully in front of me.

Somewhere down the block a car horn honked, interrupting the eerie silence.

I hoped no car would drive by.

I stopped beside the low concrete stoop. My heart was pounding so hard, I could hear it.

I climbed onto the first step and raised the test tube. *Hurry! Hurry!* I urged myself silently.

I reached a trembling hand to pull off the cork top—and the porch light came on.

chapter

16

"Oh!" I cried out in shock.

The test tube tumbled from my hand.

It shattered on the concrete stoop.

I turned and bolted for the safety of the evergreen shrubs.

Behind me, I heard the front door open.

"Who's there?" Mr. Northwood's angry, shrill voice broke through the silence.

I dived behind the shrub, joining the others.

And then I heard Mr. Northwood let out a groan of disgust. "Oh, my heavens!" he exclaimed weakly. I heard him utter a curse. And then the front door was slammed shut.

My new friends immediately moved to congratulate me. Zack wrapped me in a tight bear hug. "Johanna—you were *awesome!*" he whispered.

"You were great!" Dennis told me, grinning.

We were all laughing, slapping each other high-fives, celebrating silently behind the evergreens.

Did Mr. Northwood see me? I wondered, glancing toward the front stoop. Does he know who it was?

Our celebration didn't last long. The disgusting, sour stench traveled fast.

We all breathed it in at the same time. It was so *gross!*

I never smelled *anything* as sickening as this. My stomach lurched. I thought I was going to heave!

"We're *out* of here!" Dennis cried.

"Let's get something to eat!" Zack urged.

We piled into Melody's parents' Mercedes, and a few seconds later, backed down the driveway and roared off down Fear Street.

Zack, Lanny, Caitlin, and I somehow squeezed in the back. Dennis rode in the front beside Melody. It was really uncomfortable, but I didn't care. I had never ridden in a Mercedes before!

We laughed and joked all the way to The Corner. We were all so happy that Mission Skunk Juice had been a success.

The restaurant was nearly empty. Shadyside High students usually hung out there till all hours on weekends. But this was a school night. We squeezed into a booth near the back and all ordered hamburgers and french fries.

Zack offered to pay for mine, which was a great relief since I didn't have any money with me.

I was so happy. Here I was with the most popular kids at Shadyside. And they were all being so nice to me. I really was part of their crowd.

Caitlin made sure that she sat next to Dennis. I was unhappy about that. But Dennis kept flashing me secret smiles. And I was thrilled to be the star of the evening.

"Did you see the look on Northwood's face when he smelled the skunk juice?" Zack cried ecstatically.

"No. I was running too fast!" I admitted.

"His hair *really* stood up on end!" Caitlin declared.

"Glad I don't sit in the front row in his class," Melody said, holding her nose. "His clothes will probably stink for a month too!"

We all laughed and joked and had a great time.

It was nearly ten-thirty when they dropped me off in front of my house. I turned and waved as the silver Mercedes rolled away.

I was smiling to myself, thinking about my triumph, as I made my way up the driveway.

But my smile quickly faded when a dark figure stepped out to meet me.

chapter

17

Mr. Northwood!

That was my first thought.

Thank goodness I was wrong.

"Johanna!" Margaret called. She stepped up to me on the driveway. I saw that she carried an aluminum pot in her hands.

"Margaret, what are you doing here?" I cried.

Even in the darkness I could see the accusing glare of her eyes. "You said you had the flu, Johanna."

"Yeah. Well . . ."

A sour aroma rose on the wet night air. Skunk smell.

"Ooh. What's that?" Margaret twisted her features in disgust.

"It's a long story," I said. I led her into the house. The lights were on. I could hear Mom moving around in the back.

I called to her that I was home. Then I turned to

Margaret. She wore a pink down parka, a hand-me-down from her cousin. The hood flopped awkwardly behind her head. Her carrot-colored hair was disheveled, and it clashed with the pink coat.

She raised the pot to me. "I brought you chicken soup. My mom had some in the freezer. You said you had the flu."

"I'm sorry—" I began to say.

"You could have told me you had other plans," Margaret interrupted shrilly. "You didn't have to lie to me."

"I didn't really have plans," I said. Pretty lame.

I could see the hurt in Margaret's eyes. "If you didn't want to study with me tonight, you should've just said so, Johanna."

"You're right," I said, taking the soup from her. "I'm sorry. Dennis came over and—"

"You don't belong with them," she said bitterly.

"Huh?" Her words caught me by surprise.

"They're different from us," Margaret continued, staring hard at me. "They're used to doing whatever they want. They don't care who they hurt."

"You're being a little dramatic, aren't you?" I shot back. "You've been watching too many soaps, Margaret."

"I'm right," Margaret said. "You'll be sorry."

"Thanks, Mom," I said sarcastically.

"Enjoy the soup," Margaret said. "See you around."

She turned quickly and hurried out the door.

* * *

In the weeks to come, Dennis and his friends started hanging out at my house. They would come over after dinner, and we'd kid around and have a lot of laughs and study together.

My house wasn't as big or as fancy as theirs. But I think they liked hanging out there because there were no parents around. Since my mom was almost always at work, we had the house to ourselves.

I spent a lot of time daydreaming about Dennis, trying to figure out how I could make him dump Caitlin for good and start going out with me.

Most everyone was still having trouble with Mr. Northwood. I think he suspected that Dennis and his friends were responsible for the skunk juice attack. And so he was meaner than ever to them.

He gave both Dennis and Zack failing grades for the term. That meant that Dennis was no longer eligible for the track team. Dennis's parents came to school and argued with Mr. Hernandez. But this time the principal backed up Mr. Northwood.

Mr. Northwood also made Caitlin and Melody come in for an hour after school every day for a week—just because they were laughing together during a class discussion. And he threatened to keep us all from going on our spring class trip if our projects weren't handed in on time.

So, as the days went by, we continued to joke about how we wanted to murder Mr. Northwood.

And then, late on a Thursday night, it stopped being a joke.

* * *

Zack had sneaked two six-packs of beer from his house, and we were all sipping from the cans as we did our homework, sprawled around my living room.

I was slumped in the armchair, trying to concentrate on *Hamlet*. Dennis and Caitlin were at opposite ends of the couch, scribbling in their chemistry notebooks. Zack, Lanny, and Melody were on their stomachs on the carpet, immersed in different books.

I heard Dennis mutter something about needing a pencil, but I didn't see him get up or walk over to the little green table against the wall.

I glanced up in time to see him pull open the drawer. "Wow!" His eyes went wide as he reached in and pulled out the little pistol. "Wow! We really *could* kill Mr. Northwood!" Dennis exclaimed.

"Dennis—put that away!" Caitlin cried from the couch. She immediately sounded very frightened.

"What's that?" Lanny called, glancing up from the floor.

"We could shoot him. We really could!" Dennis cried with surprising enthusiasm.

I saw him click the bullet cartridge into the handle.

"Dennis—whoa," I said, closing my book. I had a tight feeling in my chest, a feeling of dread.

"Hey, Zack, check this out!" Dennis cried, ignoring me. He tossed the loaded pistol across the room to Zack.

Zack reached up and caught it, spilling his beer on the carpet. He didn't seem to notice. He rolled the silver pistol around in his hands, examining it carefully. "Is it real?" he asked me. "I've never held a real gun before."

"My dad left it," I explained. "For protection. Put it away—okay?"

"Yeah. Put it away. Come on!" Caitlin pleaded.

But Zack handed it to Lanny. Lanny pretended to shoot Dennis. Dennis grabbed his chest and staggered to the floor.

The boys laughed. The girls didn't.

I jumped to my feet. "Come on, guys. Stop messing around with that. You're scaring me. You really are."

"I'm leaving," Melody said tensely. She slammed her book shut and stood up. "If you don't put that away, I'm leaving. This is just stupid."

Lanny had tossed down three beers. His eyes were kind of watery. He grinned at Melody. Then he spun the pistol on his finger. "Always wanted to be a cowboy," he murmured.

"We could shoot Northwood," Dennis said, scratching his head. "It would be so easy." He crossed the room and took the pistol from Lanny.

"Bye," Melody said. "I'm serious. I'm leaving." She started toward the front hall.

Dennis carried the pistol to the window. He aimed it out at the darkness and pretended to fire it. "Bang. You're dead, Mr. Northwood," he said, grinning.

He tossed the pistol to Zack. "What do you think, man?"

Zack missed. The gun bounced on the carpet, stopping at his feet.

"Put it away! *Please!*" I shouted.

"We shoot Northwood. Then we hide the gun," Dennis said. "Then we pretend like nothing happened. No one is going to suspect a group of nice, respectable teenagers like us."

"You're crazy, Dennis," Caitlin said shrilly. "You're really crazy."

Zack aimed the gun at Lanny. "Bang. Gotcha!"

"Give me that!" Lanny demanded. Zack tossed the gun to him. Lanny examined it again. He looked up at me. "Killer gun!" he exclaimed.

"Is that supposed to be a joke?" I asked. I walked over and tried to swipe it from his hands. But he tossed it back to Dennis.

Dennis bobbled it. Nearly dropped it. Then he twirled it on his finger.

"Dennis—please!" Melody begged from the doorway.

"Watch this," Dennis said, grinning at me. "Watch the quick draw."

"No. Please!" I cried.

Ignoring me, Dennis slid the pistol into his jeans pocket. "At the count of three," he said, his green eyes flashing excitedly.

He counted to three.

Then he grabbed for the gun cowboy-style and drew it from his pocket.

We all gasped when it went off.

It sounded like the loudest firecracker.

And then Zack let out an agonized scream.

I gaped in open-mouthed horror as the bright blood

spread over the shoulder of his shirt, a small circle at first, growing bigger, bigger . . .

Zack let out another frightened scream, weaker this time.

Then, clutching his bleeding shoulder, he dropped to his knees. His eyes rolled up in his head, and he slumped heavily forward onto the carpet.

chapter

18

"*H*elp me!" Zack groaned. "Get a doctor. The blood . . . it's . . ." He grimaced in pain and shut his eyes.

The bright circle of blood spread over the shoulder of his shirt. Blood trickled to the carpet.

"Please . . ." Zack moaned, his eyes still shut.

We were all in a panic.

Caitlin had her hands pressed against her cheeks. She was panting loudly, shaking her head, large tears rolling down her face. "Do something! He's going to die!" she shrieked. "He's going to die!"

Lanny stood frozen in the center of the room, his eyes wide with fear.

"Ohh, I—I feel sick," Melody murmured, her face as white as a sheet. She started running to the hallway. But she didn't make it to the bathroom. She got as far as the front entryway and started puking her guts out.

I was as panicked as everyone else. I stood staring down at Zack, screaming, "Call an ambulance! Call an ambulance!" in a high-pitched, shrill voice. But in my horror, I made no attempt to get to the phone.

Melody was retching loudly in the front hall. Caitlin was sobbing, tugging at handfuls of her short brown hair. Lanny hadn't moved from the center of the room.

"You shot him! You shot him! Don't let him die!" Caitlin wailed.

Only Dennis remained able to think clearly. I saw his green eyes narrow as he stared down at Zack. He still gripped the pistol in one hand. He raised his eyes to mine and gestured with it.

"Call 911," Dennis instructed me. "Hurry. Get the police and an ambulance."

Dennis's voice was calm and low. His cool manner helped to steady me a little. I obediently made my way to the phone on the table in front of the window.

"Zack—can you walk?" I heard Dennis ask. "Can you stand up? Get up, Zack."

I called the emergency number. I told them there'd been a shooting. I gave them my address. I was starting to think clearly again. My heart was still racing. My hands were as cold as ice. But my mind was starting to work.

When I turned around, I saw Dennis and Lanny helping Zack toward the front door. There was a dark puddle of blood on the carpet where Zack had fallen.

"No! Don't move him!" I cried.

"We have to. I have an idea!" Dennis snapped at me.

"Stop the bleeding!" Caitlin screamed. "Stop the bleeding! He's going to die!"

"Clean up the blood—quick!" Dennis ordered me. He and Lanny were dragging Zack toward the door. Zack groaned in pain.

"Dennis, I don't understand! Where are you taking him?" I asked, totally confused.

"You'll see," Dennis replied tensely. "I have a good idea, Johanna. I'll explain later. There's no time. Just clean up the blood! Hurry!"

Zack groaned. "It . . . hurts . . . really bad."

"Don't let him die!" Caitlin shrieked. "Please don't let him die!"

Zack had his arms around the two boys' shoulders. They guided him slowly from the room. "The ambulance is coming," Lanny told Zack. "It's coming."

"Keep walking," Dennis told him. "Can you walk? Keep going, man."

They made their way past Melody, who was leaning against the wall, holding her stomach with one hand. Her blond hair had fallen over her face. She was struggling to catch her breath.

"Don't move him! He's bleeding too much!" Caitlin called in panic.

"Help Johanna clean up," Dennis ordered her. "It'll be okay. Trust me. Trust me."

Caitlin and I stared quizzically at each other. What on earth could Dennis be thinking of?

My mind was spinning. I couldn't think clearly at all. I kept hearing the gun go off, kept seeing the circle of blood grow wider on Zack's shirt.

I'll listen to Dennis, I decided.

Dennis has a plan. Dennis has an idea.

I ran to the kitchen to get sponges and a mop and soap. Caitlin followed close behind. I don't think she wanted to be alone.

"What is Dennis doing?" she asked me in a tiny frightened voice. "Zack needs a doctor! A doctor! Where are they taking him? We're in such trouble. Such terrible trouble. What is Dennis *doing?*"

"I don't know," I replied, pulling open the broom closet and dragging out the cleaning supplies. "I think we have to do what he says."

"But what is Dennis *doing?*" Caitlin repeated, her eyes red and tight with terror. "What is he doing?"

We cleaned up the living room as best we could. Melody was no help at all. She was bent over in a chair, crying and holding her stomach.

As soon as we'd finished, Caitlin and I left her there and hurried outside. It was a cold, moonless night. Low black clouds made the sky darker than usual.

I heard the rising wail of sirens close by.

The police and ambulance are on their way, I thought.

Will Zack be okay? I wondered. Will they get here in time?

And then the approaching sirens reminded me that we were all in serious trouble.

My mom suddenly flashed into my mind. What would she say when she learned we'd been playing with the gun and accidentally shot Zack?

What if Zack dies? I thought. What if he bleeds to death?

Would we all be arrested for murder?

I shook my head hard, trying to force that thought from my mind.

"What are we doing out here?" I asked aloud.

As my eyes adjusted to the darkness, I saw the three boys in Mr. Northwood's yard. Zack was lying on his back in the grass. Lanny stood over him. Dennis came jogging to the driveway when he saw Caitlin and me.

"Just go along with my story," he urged us breathlessly. Even in the darkness I could see the excitement on his face.

"Where—where's the gun?" I asked.

Dennis pointed toward the house.

"I don't understand," I murmured.

The yard filled with swirling red lights. The twin sirens wailed—and then cut off. Headlights rolled over Zack, lying on the cold, hard ground with his knees slightly raised.

Mr. Northwood's porch light flashed on.

The front door opened. Mr. Northwood stepped out on the stoop. He was in a black turtleneck and baggy gray sweat pants.

"What's going on? What's happening?" the teacher shouted, anger mixed with confusion.

His shoe bumped something. He bent over. And I saw him pick up an object.

The pistol!

Red lights swirled over everything. Car doors slammed behind us.

Zack lay motionless on the lawn.

It was hard to see anything in the swirling red lights and blinding white headlights.

Two dark-uniformed police officers appeared, hands on their gun holsters. "What's happening here?" one of them demanded.

"He shot Zack!" Dennis cried, pointing at Mr. Northwood.

"Huh?" The police officer raised his eyes to the stoop. "Hey!" he screamed angrily. "You! Drop the gun! Now!"

Mr. Northwood uttered a startled cry. He let the pistol fall.

"He shot Zack!" Dennis repeated, still pointing at Mr. Northwood. "Northwood shot Zack!"

chapter

19

Dennis lowered his face to mine and kissed my cheek.

The kiss sent a shiver down the back of my neck. I turned to kiss his lips. A long, tender kiss. When it ended, I slid my hands behind his head and kissed him again.

The car windows had steamed up. I couldn't see out at all. We were alone in our own warm, private world.

Leaning over the seat, I held him close. I could smell the coconut shampoo he'd used on his hair.

"I'd better get home," I whispered. "Before Mom gets back from work. You know I'm not allowed to see you."

"Just a few more minutes," he pleaded, his eyes burning into mine.

It was two weeks later, two weeks after the terrible night Zack had been shot. Zack was okay. Miraculously, the bullet hadn't damaged anything vital in his shoulder. It would be healed completely in a few months.

But nothing was the same for any of the rest of us.

At first, the police had been ready to believe that Mr. Northwood shot Zack. His fingerprints were on the gun, after all.

But then they learned that the gun was registered to my dad. And then they saw the bloodstains on my carpet that I hadn't been able to get up.

And then the truth came out.

We had no choice. We had to tell them what really happened.

The officers drove us to the Shadyside police station. I don't remember if they charged us with a crime or not. I was so messed up. And so frightened.

Dennis's parents and the other parents got to the police station at once. I don't know how they did it, but they got the whole thing hushed up. It was all taken care of that night. The shooting never even made the newspaper.

The next day, the parents appeared at school and tried to get us all transferred from Mr. Northwood's class. But the school didn't cooperate.

Mr. Northwood didn't press charges or anything. Maybe the parents paid him something. I don't know.

We all had to continue in his history class. And now he was really on our case—mine too. He was cold and cruel, and he didn't even try to *appear* to be fair.

He piled on tons of extra homework, especially on weekends, and made us do long, boring papers the other kids didn't have to write. He gave us failing grades on exams for the stupidest reasons. All in all, he did everything he could to pay us back and make our lives miserable.

After the shooting, my mom didn't react the way I thought she would. I guess parents seldom do.

I thought she would scream and yell and get hysterical. But instead, she quietly told me how disappointed in me she was.

I think I *wanted* her to scream and yell. The hurt look in her eyes was a lot more painful than any harsh words would have been.

"Your rich friends are a bad influence," Mom said softly, wet tears brimming in her tired eyes. "I won't allow you to see any of them again." She gave me a speech about how irresponsible I was to take the gun out, and locked it away in the bottom drawer of the desk in the living room.

And so I'd been sneaking out to see Dennis ever since.

I didn't like sneaking around behind my mom's back. But I couldn't help it. I was falling in love with Dennis. And I would do anything to see him.

We would park up on River Ridge, the high cliff that overlooked town. It was a popular parking spot for Shadyside High kids, but it was so cold out, we were usually the only car up there.

Dennis and I would hold each other. And kiss— long, sweet kisses. And talk.

Mostly Dennis would talk about how Mr. Northwood was ruining his life, destroying his chances to be on the Olympic track team, and ruining his whole future.

"He's going to fail me. I know he is," Dennis would say, shaking his head unhappily. "He wants to pay us all back. He's going to flunk us all."

I wanted to say something encouraging. But I had the feeling that Dennis was right.

I loved looking at Dennis, just gazing at him, even when he was unhappy and grumbling about Mr. Northwood. I liked his dark eyebrows, the way they formed wide, upside-down V's above his deep green eyes. I liked his smooth, straight nose and his toothy smile. He looked like a little boy when he smiled.

I often thought about Dennis and how he had acted the night Zack was shot. He was so calm, so quick-thinking.

Dennis was so determined to get what he wanted. He came up with an idea. And then he made it happen.

He acted with such confidence.

I wondered what it would feel like to *be* like Dennis, to feel like you can get whatever you want. That you can do anything—and get away with it.

"We'd better get home," I whispered, wiping away a circle of steam from the passenger window with my hand. "I don't want to. But I have to."

Dennis stared straight ahead at the steamed-up windshield. He made no move to start up the car.

"What's wrong?" I asked, placing my hand tenderly on his.

"Thinking about Northwood," he muttered.

"Not tonight," I pleaded. "I mean, what can we do?"

"Lanny dared me to kill him," Dennis revealed, avoiding my eyes.

"Huh?" I wasn't sure I heard right.

"Lanny dared me to," Dennis repeated. He squeezed my hand between both of his. "Then I dared Zack to do it." He snickered, as if he had just made a joke.

"Zack's still all bandaged up," I murmured.

"We were all daring each other to do it," Dennis said, shaking his head. "In study hall."

He turned to me. I saw that his chin was trembling.

Is he going to *cry?* I wondered, startled.

"I—I can't let Northwood wreck my whole life!" he declared in a trembling voice. "Somebody has to do something about him. Somebody has to!"

His eyes burned into mine.

I'm not sure why, but I think I loved him more than ever at that moment.

I wanted him to be mine. All mine. I didn't want to share him with Caitlin anymore.

I wanted to be *with* him. And I wanted to be *like* him.

"Maybe I should dare *you* to kill him," Dennis teased, tenderly moving his finger down the side of my face. "You've always wanted to be included in our stupid dares, haven't you?"

"Maybe," I replied coyly, smiling back at him.

"Well, maybe I should dare *you,*" he repeated, his eyes flashing.

"Go ahead. Try me," I whispered, grabbing his hand.

His expression turned solemn. His eyes burned into mine. "I dare you to kill Northwood," he said.

"Okay," I replied, feeling my heart pound in my chest. "I'll do it."

chapter

20

"Good luck, Johanna."

I turned from my locker to see who was talking to me.

A girl with blond hair tied in a long, thick braid flashed me a smile. "Good luck," she repeated.

"Huh?" I just stared at her. I didn't know what she was talking about. Then, slowly, it dawned on me. She was wishing me good luck on the dare—good luck on killing Mr. Northwood!

Hey, I'm getting famous! I thought. I wasn't sure if I was happy about it or not.

It was the following Monday. I had the feeling that kids were staring at me, talking about me all down the hall.

I slammed the locker shut and started to class, when I felt a hand touch my back. "Oh, hi, Margaret," I said, turning to face her.

I hadn't seen much of Margaret lately. I knew she

didn't approve of Dennis and my other new friends. She and I just didn't have much in common anymore.

"Johanna—what's going on?" Margaret demanded. She had a fretful frown on her face, and she looked me up and down as if searching for fleas.

"Not much," I replied casually. "What's up?"

"Don't pretend," Margaret scolded. "I want to know what is going on."

She grabbed my arm and dragged me into the girls' bathroom. She was breathing hard and kept staring at my face as if trying to find some hidden secrets there.

Suki Thomas was putting on lipstick in front of the mirror. Then Suki started brushing her bleached-blond hair.

Margaret stared at me without speaking, waiting for Suki to leave.

"I've got to go," I said impatiently, shifting my backpack to the other shoulder.

"Just wait," Margaret replied. Suki finally left. She flashed me a wink as she passed by and gave me a thumbs-up. I hoped Margaret hadn't caught it.

I didn't really want to discuss the dare with Margaret. I knew she wouldn't understand. I wasn't sure I understood myself.

But I guess it was too late to play innocent.

"The whole school is talking about you!" Margaret declared.

It was supposed to be an accusation. But I have to admit I liked the idea of everyone talking about me. It was kind of exciting to be some kind of celebrity just once in my life.

"They say you accepted a dare," Margaret continued, pushing a strand of red hair off her freckled forehead. "To kill Mr. Northwood. Everyone's talking about it. But it isn't true—is it?"

I hesitated. I could see how upset she was.

"No. No way," I muttered, avoiding her accusing eyes.

"Then why are Zack and Lanny taking bets?" Margaret demanded.

"Huh? They are?" My surprise was genuine. No one had told me that any bets were being made. I have to admit I was really shocked to hear about it.

The bell rang.

"Margaret—we're going to be late," I said, edging toward the door.

She stepped in front of me and blocked my escape. "They're taking bets. Everyone is betting on whether you'll do it or not. This is crazy, Johanna. It really is. It's crazy!"

"Yeah," I agreed. "Yeah, it is. It's crazy."

Margaret is right, I told myself, sitting in math class, staring out the window at a gray day. A light snow was falling, wet snowflakes clinging silently to the window-pane.

It's crazy. The whole idea is crazy. There's no way I'm going through with this. No way.

It had seemed like such a romantic thing to say that night up on River Ridge. It was so exciting to be up there with Dennis. I wanted to make him happy. I wanted so desperately for him to like me.

But I'd had a lot of time to think about it. In fact, I hadn't been able to think about anything else.

And I knew I couldn't do it.

I looked for Dennis after school. I had to tell him. I had to tell him the dare was off.

But I couldn't find him.

Lanny came running up to me in the hall. "Over a thousand dollars," he whispered excitedly, grinning at me. "Do you believe it?"

"Huh?" I stared back at him, trying to figure out what he was telling me.

"A thousand dollars so far," he repeated, whispering. "And you get half of it."

"I do? I didn't realize—"

"If you-know-what happens to you-know-who," Lanny added.

"But, wait—" I cried. I wanted to tell him he had to return the money.

"Got to run!" Lanny cried, trotting away. "Later!" He disappeared around the corner.

Five hundred dollars? I thought. I'd never had that kind of money in my life. I'd never *seen* five hundred dollars!

I looked down at the big moth hole on the sleeve of my sweater. Five hundred dollars could buy a few new sweaters, I thought wistfully.

But it was crazy. So totally crazy.

I wasn't killing Mr. Northwood for the money. I was killing him to help Dennis. Just for Dennis.

Dennis had dared me.

And you can't wimp out on a dare.

And—whoa! Whoa, girl!

What was I *thinking?*

THE DARE

I couldn't do it—I couldn't kill Mr. Northwood even if I wanted to—*could* I?

That night Mom was home early for once. We had a pretty nice dinner together. I forced myself not to think about the dare and all that was going on at school over it.

When Mom asked me what was happening at school, I made up some things about class projects and the annual talent show. I felt guilty lying, but what could I do? I couldn't tell her what was really on my mind.

The phone rang a little after seven. I ran to pick it up. I didn't want Mom to get there first in case it was Dennis.

And it was.

"Dennis, Mom's home," I whispered. "I can't talk."

"Saturday," he said. "The bets are all for Saturday. I'm counting on you, Johanna." Then he hung up.

I stared out the kitchen window at Mr. Northwood's backyard. The late afternoon sun had drifted behind large gray clouds. Yesterday's snow had stopped after a few hours, leaving only a powdery film over the grass and bare trees.

Two enormous black crows had perched on top of the tall woodpile in the center of Mr. Northwood's yard. They were bobbing their heads and cawing loudly. They seemed to be having some kind of argument.

When Mr. Northwood appeared in the yard, zipping up his red and black plaid wool coat, the crows gave a startled cry and flapped away.

I watched Mr. Northwood as he pulled a red wool ski cap over his bushy gray hair. Then he made his way to the woodpile. It was stacked so high, so many logs, it rose up over his head.

He bent down and picked up a couple of logs from a lower stack. Then, bundling them in his arms, he started back to his house.

I swallowed hard. I had a sudden idea.

Maybe I wouldn't have to shoot Mr. Northwood.

Maybe I could kill him another way and make it look like an accident.

"Yes!" I cried aloud, so excited my legs were trembling. "Yes!"

I heard his kitchen storm door slam. He disappeared into his house.

I ran outside. I didn't stop to get my coat. I knew I didn't have much time.

I had watched Mr. Northwood bring wood into the house before. He always carried two logs at a time. He always made three or four trips.

I knew he would be back out for two more logs in a matter of seconds.

I took a deep breath of the frozen air and started to run. I prayed he wouldn't see me.

I had to get behind the woodpile before he returned.

My legs felt as if they weighed a thousand pounds. Halfway across his backyard, I glanced at his house. No sign of him.

With a desperate gasp I forced my legs to move.

Got to get there. Got to get there!

I practically dived behind the tall wall of logs as I heard Mr. Northwood's kitchen door slam again.

Keeping low behind the woodpile, I struggled to catch my breath, listening to him humming softly to himself as he returned for more logs.

Could I do it? Could I?

The timing had to be just right.

I heard his footsteps. His humming grew louder. I knew he was just about at the woodpile now.

I tensed both hands. I raised them above my head and placed them against the rough wall of logs.

I suddenly felt weak, so weak, as if all my muscles were melting away.

No! I told myself.

Don't give in to that. Don't weaken.

Mr. Northwood was on the other side of the woodpile. I could hear his whistling breaths. I could hear the scrape of his corduroy trouser legs.

So close. So close.

I heard him let out a soft groan as he bent over to pick up logs.

And I heaved against the tall woodpile with all my might. I shoved against it with both hands and then my entire body.

The logs toppled forward.

Yes!

I heard Mr. Northwood's startled cry.

The logs dropped onto him, buried him beneath them.

He uttered a curse and then cried out in pain.

I stepped around to see him struggling to climb out.

I froze as he stared up at me, his blue eyes cold and angry. I was disappointed. I had expected logs to fall on his head, to knock him out.

But he called out my name. He shoved a log off his chest and started to climb to his feet.

"No," I said aloud. "No, no." I couldn't allow that. He wasn't supposed to climb out.

I lifted a heavy log off the tangle of logs. It was covered with dark brown bark and had a sharp point on one side where a branch had been broken off.

"No, no, no."

I swung the log down as hard as I could on top of his red wool ski cap.

A loud *oof* escaped his mouth. His skull made a disgusting sound as it cracked open.

Then his mouth dropped open, and his blue eyes spun wildly like marbles in his head.

Blood poured down from under the cap, like a red waterfall over his face.

Then his head dropped back, and his entire body sprawled backward onto the logs.

"Yuck. What a mess!" I whispered, shaking my head.

The sound of his skull cracking kept repeating in my mind. I wondered if I would ever be able to crack open an egg without thinking of Mr. Northwood.

With a shudder, I bent over him and placed my finger under his nose. I kept it there for several seconds, until I was sure he wasn't breathing.

Then I started picking up logs and arranging them on top of his body. I dropped the bloody one onto his face. I piled two or three more over his chest.

My heart was pounding as I stepped back to admire my work.

Did it look like an accident?

Yes.

What a terrible accident. Poor Mr. Northwood was killed when his woodpile collapsed on top of him.

That's what everyone would say.

Poor Mr. Northwood.

I took a last look, dropped one more log over his chest, and hurried to the house to call Dennis with the good news.

chapter

22

That was another of my frightening fantasies.

Staring out my kitchen window at the woodpile, I imagined the whole scene with Mr. Northwood.

If only it were true, I thought.

If only I didn't have to shoot him.

It was Thursday afternoon, and I had stayed home from school. My stomach was upset. I felt really shaky and strange. I was a nervous wreck.

The alarm had gone off at seven, the usual time. I had started to get dressed—and then realized I couldn't face another day at school, another day of kids staring at me, wishing me good luck, asking me when I was going to shoot him.

At first, I had loved all the attention.

But now it frightened me.

After my mom went off to work, I climbed back into

bed. I was shaking all over. I couldn't get rid of my chills. Finally I fell back to sleep and didn't wake up until noon.

I kept getting painful stomachaches. And I felt like I had to puke. I forced down some buttered toast and a Coke for lunch, but then my stomach felt even worse.

Maybe I'm sick, I thought. Maybe I really do have the flu.

But I knew I was just scared to death about killing Mr. Northwood.

Once he's dead, I'll feel so much better. That's what I told myself. Strange way to cheer oneself up, huh?

I should have worked on my research project. But I knew I couldn't concentrate.

I didn't waste the day, though. I found a good hiding place for the pistol. There is a loose stone in the basement wall behind the dryer. After I shoot Mr. Northwood, I'll pull the stone out and slip the gun into the hole. The gun will fit snugly behind the stone, and no one will ever find it.

Finding that hiding place made me feel a little better. But just a little bit.

Dennis called at three-thirty. He saw that I wasn't in school and wondered if I was okay.

I thought it was sweet of him to call. He's really starting to care about me, I thought.

"We've collected nearly twelve hundred dollars," he told me, lowering his voice to a whisper. I could picture his green eyes sparkling with excitement.

"Wow" was all I managed to reply. I mean, it was impressive. That's a lot of money.

"Half of it is yours," Dennis continued, "if—"

"Shhhhh." I cut him off. "I don't care about the money. I really don't." ˙

"But you're still doing it, right?" Dennis asked. I caught a little worry in his voice.

"Yeah. Sure," I replied reluctantly.

"Saturday," Dennis repeated. "Saturday."

I didn't want him to hang up. I wanted to talk longer. I wanted him to tell me that he was dumping Caitlin, that he was interested only in me now. I wanted him to tell me how brave I was, how much I was helping him, how much fun we were going to have together once . . . once Mr. Northwood was dead.

But Dennis muttered good-bye, and the dial tone buzzed in my ear.

As I replaced the receiver, Dennis's low voice echoed in my ear. *"Saturday . . . Saturday . . . Saturday . . ."*

I heard sounds in the backyard. Making my way to the kitchen window, I saw Mr. Northwood. Home from school. In his red and black flannel jacket and wool ski cap. Bending over to pick up logs from his woodpile.

That's when I had the evil fantasy of pushing the logs onto him and bashing in his skull and making it look like a terrible accident.

My daydream ended. Mr. Northwood was still standing there in the middle of his backyard.

And as I stared at him, bundling two logs in his arms and starting to the house with them, I realized I was shaking all over.

"I can't take this!" I cried aloud.

I knew that I'd never make it to Saturday. Never.

My heart pounding, I walked quickly to the desk in the living room to get the gun. I untaped the key my mother hid under the desk and slid it into the keyhole.

I'm going to do it now, I decided.

chapter
23

My hand was trembling as I pulled open the drawer and reached for the gun. But I stopped shaking as soon as my hand wrapped around the pistol.

Something about how solid it was made me feel calmer.

It felt so warm in my cold, clammy hand. Warm and almost . . . comforting.

I dragged my coat out of the front closet and pulled it on. Then I slipped the gun into a coat pocket.

I'm going to feel so much better in just a few moments, I told myself.

I peered out through the window in the kitchen door. Mr. Northwood was bending over in front of the woodpile, arranging logs, his back to me.

I opened the kitchen door and stepped out onto the back stoop. I had my right hand inside the coat pocket, wrapped tightly around the pistol.

I'm going to feel so much better.

It was a bone-chillingly cold day, but I couldn't feel it. I didn't feel anything except the pistol in my hand.

I didn't see anything except Mr. Northwood bent over his logs.

I made my way across my backyard, stepping carefully over the frozen ground, being careful not to make a sound.

How close do I need to get? I asked myself, staring hard at Mr. Northwood's red and black wool back.

How close? How close?

Close enough not to miss.

I stopped short when he stood up.

Was he going to turn around and see me? Was he going to spoil this for me?

He stretched, pushing his long arms straight up over his head. Then he bent again and began lifting logs onto a low stack.

I pulled the gun from my coat pocket. I was squeezing it so tightly, my hand hurt.

I pulled back the hammer. It made a metallic *click*.

I sucked in my breath, afraid Mr. Northwood had heard it.

He let out a groan as he dropped some logs onto the stack he was building.

I took another step toward him, tiptoeing on the frozen grass. Another step.

How close do I have to get? How close?

Another step. Another.

I raised the gun, aimed it at his back.

Am I *really* doing this? I suddenly wondered. Am I

really crossing the backyard with a loaded pistol in my hand?

Am I really going to shoot Mr. Northwood?

Or is this another one of my violent fantasies?

No.

This was no fantasy. This was real.

Cold and real.

I aimed for his back, slid my finger over the trigger, and prepared to shoot.

chapter

24

"Johanna!"

I gasped as I heard a girl shout my name.

Mr. Northwood heard her too. He spun around, startled.

Had he seen the gun before I jammed it back into my coat pocket?

"Johanna, I didn't hear you!" he cried, his blue eyes wide with surprise.

"I—I came to ask you about the homework," I stammered, thinking quickly.

I turned to see who had called out my name. "Margaret!" She was standing in the driveway, her bulging backpack slung over the shoulder of her coat. "What are *you* doing here?" I demanded.

"There's going to be a quiz tomorrow," she replied, making her way across the grass. "You weren't there. I thought maybe you'd need the notes."

"What a considerate friend," Mr. Northwood commented. "Where were you today, Johanna? We missed you."

"I didn't feel well," I told him.

He *tsk-tsked* and returned to his logs. Margaret and I began heading back toward my house.

"I have a tape recording of the class, if you'd like to hear what you missed," Mr. Northwood called to me.

I thanked him but said I'd borrow Margaret's notes instead.

"Do you want to come in?" I asked Margaret. I was studying her face, trying to figure out why she had come. She and I hadn't been friendly for weeks. I knew she hadn't come to deliver the history notes.

"No. I have only a minute," she replied. She brushed a ringlet of red hair off her forehead.

The afternoon sun lowered behind the trees. A shadow rolled over both of us. The air grew colder.

"Everyone's talking about you, Johanna," Margaret whispered, gazing over my shoulder to Mr. Northwood. "Everyone's talking about the dare and about all the money that kids are betting."

"Yeah . . . well . . ." What was I supposed to say?

I had a sudden impulse to explain it all to Margaret. I really wanted to tell her how Mr. Northwood was ruining Dennis's whole life and how he was picking only on Dennis's friends, and how he was ruining my life too.

But I knew Margaret wouldn't understand about Dennis and me. She would never understand about the dare or about Dennis and me and the kids in our group, because Margaret wasn't one of us.

She wouldn't get it. She just wouldn't.

So I fought back the impulse to explain and just returned her stare.

"So what do you want?" I asked sharply.

She hesitated, chewing her lower lip. "Well . . . I just had to ask you," she said, her voice nearly a whisper. "I mean . . . you're not really going through with it—are you?"

"No. Of course not," I told her, squeezing the gun tightly inside my coat pocket. "Of course not."

chapter

25

Saturday arrived gray and blustery.

A perfect day for a murder, I thought, staring down at the bare maple trees from my bedroom window.

I stayed in bed until I heard the car door slam and heard Mom drive off to work. Then I quickly got cleaned up and dressed, pulling on gray sweats. I brushed and brushed my hair until my scalp hurt. I think I needed some pain to wake me up.

It was nearly lunchtime, but I couldn't eat. I paced around nervously, walking from room to room like a caged lion.

My stomach was churning. My throat felt so tight, I could barely swallow.

This is crazy, I thought. Crazy.

Mr. Northwood probably won't even be home.

I gazed out the kitchen window. No sign of him. The woodpile stood darkly in the center of the gray yard, like a hulking animal.

A scrawny squirrel stood tensely to the left of it, its tail straight up in the air. A loud *bang,* a car backfiring, I think, made the squirrel dash frantically for safety.

I had to laugh. That squirrel looks like I feel! I told myself.

My stomach started to ache. I felt really sick.

I began pacing again. One room blurred darkly into the next.

Without realizing where I was going or what I was doing, I found myself in the basement. I was reaching behind the dryer, pulling out the loose stone in the wall, checking once again the place I was going to hide the gun after I had used it.

Saturday afternoon. It was Saturday afternoon.

Saturday. Saturday. Saturday.

I repeated the word over and over until it had no meaning, until it made no sense.

Until *nothing* made sense.

And then back up in the kitchen, leaning on the windowsill, I saw Mr. Northwood appear in his backyard. His red and black wool coat was open, revealing a green turtleneck underneath. His gray hair stood up on his head, fluttering in the strong breeze.

He carried an open can of paint in one hand, a fat paintbrush in the other.

My heart pounding, I watched him make his way to the shed behind his garage, his head bobbing as he took his usual long strides.

He's going to paint the shed, I realized, pressing my hot forehead against the cool windowpane. He's going to paint the shed in his backyard.

And I'm going to shoot him.

Because it's Saturday Saturday Saturday Saturday.

And nothing makes sense.

My stomach churned. I pictured waves of molten lava rolling around inside me. I'm a volcano, I thought, about to erupt.

I swallowed hard, trying to force back my nausea.

I was in the living room now. I glanced down and saw the pistol gripped in my hand.

How did it get there?

I didn't remember walking from the kitchen. I didn't remember crossing the living room, opening the table drawer, lifting the gun.

But I had.

I had the pistol in my hand now.

Because it was Saturday Saturday Saturday.

And Mr. Northwood was in his backyard. Waiting to be killed.

Holding the pistol in one hand, I rubbed my aching stomach with the other. Then I started to the closet to get my coat.

And the doorbell rang.

chapter

26

Startled, I dropped the gun. It hit the carpet and bounced toward the couch.

The doorbell rang again.

The sound sent a chill down my back.

With a low groan, I bent and grabbed the gun. I stuffed it back into the drawer, pushed the drawer shut, and hurried to see who was at the front door.

"Dennis!"

He didn't smile. His eyes burned into mine. "Did you do it?"

"Not yet," I said. I stepped back so he could get into the house. "I—I'm not sure I can," I admitted.

He didn't seem to hear me. "Is Northwood home?"

I nodded. "In the backyard. Painting his shed. Do you believe it? He picks the coldest day of the year to paint."

"That's great!" Dennis exclaimed, his eyes studying me.

"What are you doing here?" I demanded.

"You're not very friendly," he replied, pretending to pout.

"I'm a little nervous," I told him. "And my stomach—"

He interrupted me by moving forward and pressing his lips against mine. His face was cold from the outside, but his mouth was warm.

"That was for moral support," he said when the kiss had ended.

I trembled. My entire body was shaking. I felt as if I were made of rubber, as if I had no bones at all.

"Let's get it over with," Dennis whispered in my ear, "so we can celebrate."

"Celebrate," I repeated numbly. That word didn't make any sense either.

Nothing made sense. Nothing.

"Where's the gun?" Dennis demanded, staring intensely into my eyes.

I pointed to the drawer in the green table.

My stomach churned. "I'll be right back," I told him, rubbing it with one hand over my gray sweatsuit.

"Where are you going?" he asked shrilly. I could see that he was nervous too. Beads of perspiration formed a glistening line across his forehead.

"Just upstairs. I need to get some medicine. For my stomach. You know. The pink stuff."

I hurried up the stairs, feeling dizzy and about to puke. I dived into the bathroom and slammed the door shut.

I splashed cold water on my face and forced my

breathing to slow down. Then I took a long swig of the pink stuff.

I don't know how long I stood there, leaning over the sink, staring at my pale, frightened face in the medicine chest mirror, waiting for my stomach to stop churning and aching.

I heard another car backfire somewhere outside.

I heard the wind rattle our old bathroom window.

I splashed more cold water on my hot face.

I wanted to stay up there. I didn't want to go back down. But I knew I had to.

Because it was Saturday Saturday Saturday.

And I had accepted a dare. And you can't wimp out on a dare.

I made my way downstairs on rubbery legs. My stomach still ached, but I forced myself to ignore it.

"You okay?" Dennis demanded, eyeing me with concern. His entire forehead glistened with sweat now. And he had bright beads of sweat over his upper lip.

He looks as pale as I do, I realized. He seems just as tense and afraid.

That's so sweet, I thought. He cares about me. Dennis really cares about me.

Somehow his being nervous for me gave me new strength. I crossed the living room and pulled the pistol from the drawer. Again it felt so warm wrapped inside my cold, wet hand.

"Good luck, Johanna," Dennis whispered. I felt his warm breath on my ear.

I hesitated at the kitchen door. I wanted to kiss him. I wanted to kiss him for a long, long time.

There will be time for that . . . after.

That's what I told myself as I stepped outside.

It was so gray, so dark. The sky seemed to hover right over my head. The air was cold but dry.

Standing on the back stoop, the pistol gripped tightly in my hand inside my coat pocket, I raised my eyes to Mr. Northwood's backyard.

I looked for him first at the shed. But to my surprise, he had moved to the woodpile. He seemed to be leaning over a stack of logs. Rearranging them, I guessed.

I sucked in a deep breath and began moving quickly, silently, across the grass.

The pistol was burning hot in my hand.

The dark sky appeared to whir by overhead. The ground rolled beneath my sneakers. The grass appeared to buckle and bend. The tree trunks shimmied as if made of rubber.

Everything moved. Everything roared past me. The ground, the sky, the bare trees. The wind.

I shut my eyes, blinked several times, opened them again, trying to force the world to return to normal.

Normal?

This was Saturday.

Not a normal day. A day when nothing made sense.

Mr. Northwood leaned over the pile of logs. His arms were outstretched. The back of his coat glared at me like a target.

I pulled the pistol from my pocket.
I clicked back the hammer.
I slipped my finger over the trigger.
I stepped closer. Closer.
Could I do it?
Could I?

chapter

27

I tried to aim for the middle of Mr. Northwood's back.

But the gun began to shake in my hand.

I gripped it with *both* hands, trying to hold it steady.

Mr. Northwood's wool coat flapped behind him in a sudden gust of wind.

I knew I had to shoot. Now. Before he climbed up. Before he turned around.

Before he saw me.

I struggled to steady the gun.

Shoot it! I ordered myself. *Shoot! Shoot! Shoot!*

I *had* to shoot. Because it was Saturday.

But I couldn't shoot.

I knew I couldn't shoot.

Everything started to make sense again.

I couldn't do this, I knew.

I'm me. I'm Johanna.

I'm not a murderer. I can't shoot someone. I can't shoot *anyone*.

I'm Johanna. And everything is starting to make sense.

What was I thinking of? I asked myself. What *happened* to me?

I lowered the gun. I moved it behind my back.

I began to feel better immediately. My stomach stopped churning. My throat loosened. I began to breathe normally again.

I'm not a murderer. I'm me. I'm Johanna.

I'm not going to do it. Not!

It's Saturday. But I'm not going to kill him.

Mr. Northwood didn't move.

Everything made sense again. Except Mr. Northwood didn't move.

The wind gusted. His red and black coat flapped.

He didn't move. His arms hung limply over the stack of logs.

"Mr. Northwood?" I slipped the gun into my coat pocket. "Mr. Northwood?" My voice, weak and trembling, blew back at me in the gusting wind.

He didn't move.

I stepped closer. Closer.

I gasped when I saw the dark stain on the back of his coat. The dark purple stain.

The dark purple bloodstain.

"Mr. Northwood?"

Why didn't he answer me? Why didn't he move?

I stared at the round purple stain on the coat. As it came into focus, I saw that the stain surrounded a deep hole, a hole through the coat. A hole in Mr. Northwood's back.

Then I lowered my eyes to the dark puddle of blood on the ground in front of the woodpile.

"Mr. Northwood? Mr. Northwood?"

But of course he didn't answer me.

As I stared in open-mouthed horror, I realized that he had *already* been shot to death.

chapter

28

My knees started to shake. I fought to stay on my feet.

The gray sky seemed to lower over me, forcing me to see everything through a thick, swirling cloud.

Suddenly I became aware of footsteps behind me. I turned my head to see Dennis running across the grass, a smile on his face.

"Johanna—you did it!" he exclaimed.

"N-no," I choked out. "No, Dennis."

He stepped beside me and slid his arm heavily around my trembling shoulders. His eyes were locked on Mr. Northwood's body, sprawled facedown over the woodpile.

"You did it!" Dennis repeated happily. "I can't believe it! Wow! You did it!"

"But I didn't shoot him!" I screamed, pulling out from under Dennis's arm. "Listen to me, Dennis! I didn't do it! I didn't!"

Dennis's grin didn't fade. His green eyes flashed excitedly as he turned to me. "Of course you did, Johanna. You shot him."

"No—please! Listen to me!" I begged.

"Check out your gun," Dennis instructed calmly. "Go ahead, Johanna. Check it out."

"Huh? What do you mean?" I hesitated, staring at him through the thick gray mist that refused to lift from my eyes. "What do you mean, Dennis? Why won't you listen to me?"

"Check out your gun." He pointed to my coat pocket.

I pulled the pistol out, the pistol I had never fired. Why was Dennis insisting that I had?

"Look at it," Dennis instructed me, still grinning. "Your gun has been fired. See the powder on the barrel? Go ahead. Smell it."

I obediently sniffed the nose of the barrel. I smelled gunpowder.

The gun, I remembered, had felt so warm when I had lifted it from the drawer in the living room.

"But, Dennis, I didn't—"

"I called the police," Dennis interrupted, his smile fading, his expression turning cold.

"What?" I cried, startled.

"I called the police," he replied casually. "They'll be here any second. I'll tell them it was self-defense, Johanna. Don't worry. I'll tell them that Northwood attacked you and you fired in self-defense."

"But, Dennis, why—" I started to say. And then I stopped.

It was all making sense. Even through the thick gray

cloud that had lowered over me, it was all making sense.

The car backfire while I was upstairs in the bathroom—it wasn't a backfire.

"Dennis—*you* shot him!" I cried in a hushed, shocked voice I'd never heard before. *"You* shot him, Dennis!"

Dennis took a step back, his eyes on Mr. Northwood's body. "I'll tell them you did it in self-defense, Johanna," he said softly.

"But *you* shot him!" I shouted. "While I was in the bathroom."

I could feel my fury grow. The volcano was about to erupt. I grabbed his shoulders. "Dennis—why?"

He jerked away from me, his eyes lighting up angrily.

"Why, Dennis?" I demanded. "You set this all up, didn't you!" I accused him. "You set *me* up! Why?"

"What's happening?" A girl's voice called from the driveway.

I turned to see Caitlin hurrying over to us.

"Oh, Caitlin!" I cried, so happy to see her. "Caitlin —help me! Please?" I went running to her.

But she sidestepped me and hurried over to Dennis.

"It went perfectly," Dennis told her, grinning. He pointed down to Mr. Northwood's body.

She kissed him on the cheek. "We did it!" Caitlin cried.

chapter

29

I froze.

Caitlin slid her arm around Dennis's waist, holding him close.

The trees along the back fence suddenly came to life, their branches trembling, their slender trunks leaning in a strong burst of wind. Fat brown leaves raced over my sneakers as if trying to flee.

"I don't get this," I muttered.

"It was all a dare," Dennis explained casually. "Caitlin dared me to let you take care of our Northwood problem."

"You mean—" Too many thoughts ran through my mind at once. I felt as if my head would burst.

"It was easy to get you to volunteer," Dennis continued. "You seemed so eager. And you made it so easy too." Caitlin nodded in agreement, her eyes on Dennis.

"I could hardly believe it when it turned out that

you of all people owned a gun," he said with a laugh. "I didn't even have to try to think of a clever way to kill him. You had the perfect weapon right in your own house."

"You went out with me just because you wanted me to kill Mr. Northwood?" I demanded, ignoring the chills that ran down my back, ignoring the blood throbbing at my temples.

Dennis nodded. "Pretty much. It was a dare, see."

"Dennis is going with me," Caitlin murmured, staring hard at me. "Didn't you wonder why he was suddenly so interested in you?"

"I can't believe you planned this whole thing," I said, shaking my head unhappily.

"I have to get back on the track team," Dennis replied softly. "Northwood was ruining my whole life. You seemed so eager to take care of Northwood for me."

I let out a gasp. "But then *you* shot him. *You* killed him. Why?"

"I thought you might wimp out," Dennis replied. "I couldn't take that chance. So I did it. But the police will think you did it. Everyone will think you did it."

Something inside me exploded. The volcano went off. My anger, my hurt, burst out of me in a flood of cries and furious words.

"I trusted you! I trusted you! I cared about you!"

I heard the words escape my lips, but I didn't feel that I was saying them. I was too hurt, too broken to think clearly, too angry, too betrayed to see!

Caitlin and Dennis held on to each other. They stared back at me defiantly, coldly.

My anger and hurt meant nothing to them. Nothing.

Dennis had killed Mr. Northwood. And now I was going to be blamed.

My life was ruined so that Dennis could rejoin the track team and live happily ever after with Caitlin.

I heard sirens approaching from the street.

They blended with my own furious screams.

I was out of control. Out of myself. Out of my head.

"I can't let you do this to me!" I shrieked at Dennis.

The pistol was in my hand.

I raised it to Dennis's chest and pulled the trigger.

chapter
30

No, I didn't.

I couldn't. I'm not a killer.

I was breathing hard, gasping for air. I felt as if I were choking, drowning, going under, down, down into frightening darkness.

What was that angry wail?

Was it my desperate cry?

Was it the police siren?

Why was it so dark? So terrifyingly dark?

Why couldn't I breathe?

"Drop the gun! Drop it!" A man's stern voice broke through the darkness.

Before I could move, powerful hands grabbed me roughly. I saw a flurry of movement. Dark uniforms. Grim faces. A hand pulled the pistol away by the barrel.

"Don't move!" the man ordered.

Someone stepped behind me, grabbed my arms, and forced them behind my back.

The darkness lifted slowly.

Four police officers came into focus.

Two of them bent over Mr. Northwood. One of them held on to me tightly from behind. The other stepped up to Dennis and Caitlin.

To my surprise, I saw that Caitlin had started to cry. "It was so *horrible!*" she wailed to the solemn-faced officer.

"We saw the whole thing," Dennis said, his features tight with sorrow, his arm still around Caitlin's trembling shoulders.

Caitlin let out a sob. She took several deep breaths. "We tried to stop Johanna," she told the police officer, wiping her tears off her cheeks with her hands. "We tried to stop her. But we weren't in time."

"If only we'd arrived sooner," Dennis added, shaking his head. "Just a few seconds earlier, and Mr. Northwood would still be alive."

"But she shot him!" Caitlin cried. "Johanna shot him!"

The other officer pulled my arms up behind me until I cried out from the pain. "Read Johanna her rights," he instructed his partner. He lowered his face close to mine. "The charge will be first-degree murder."

"*H*ey—he's still alive!" one of the officers bent over Mr. Northwood declared.

"Get an ambulance unit," his partner instructed.
"He's lost a lot of blood, but he's hanging on. He can
make it if they hurry."

Mr. Northwood wasn't dead!

The good news made my heart jump as the officer
droned on, reciting my rights.

"My mother," I murmured, struggling to think
clearly. "My mother is at work."

"We'll get your mother," the officer holding my
arms said in a low, gruff voice. "And you'll need a
good attorney, miss. Even if the guy lives, you're in a
lot of serious trouble. Assault with a deadly weapon.
Intent to kill."

"But I didn't—" I choked off my words with a
defeated sob.

There was no way they would believe me.

Caitlin and Dennis had seen to that.

I could deny my guilt forever, but no one would ever listen.

The whole school knew that I was going to shoot Mr. Northwood. There were a hundred witnesses who could tell the police about the bets on whether or not I would do it.

Besides, the police didn't even need other witnesses.

They had caught me with the gun, the gun that had shot Mr. Northwood.

No one would believe I was innocent. No one.

The officer started to drag me to the police cruisers. I glanced back to see Caitlin crying her eyes out. Dennis had his arms around her, comforting her.

"Why did she shoot him? Why?" I heard Caitlin mumble through her tears.

Quite a performance.

The officer had pulled me to the driveway when we heard the other policeman's surprised cry. "Hey, Walt—come back here! Take a look at this!"

He turned me roughly around and pulled me back toward the woodpile. Dennis was still comforting Caitlin. Two officers were staring at something in their partner's hand.

"I pulled this from the victim's coat pocket," the officer said. He held up Mr. Northwood's tiny cassette recorder.

"So what?" another officer demanded.

"It's on. It's recording," his partner replied. "I'll bet we have the whole shooting on tape here."

Caitlin abruptly stopped crying. She and Dennis

stared in silent horror as the policeman pushed a button and started to rewind the cassette in the tiny recorder.

"I don't believe this!" one of the officers exclaimed.

We heard jabbering backward voices at high speed. Then the officer pushed another button, and we heard Dennis say, *"It was all a dare. Caitlin dared me to let you take care of our Northwood problem."*

No one moved. No one breathed.

"Turn it off!" Caitlin shrieked. She made a grab for the tape player. But an officer pulled her back by the waist.

Dennis let out a defeated sigh and lowered his head. Caitlin struggled to get to the recorder, but the officer held on firmly.

"You shot him," I heard myself say through the tiny tape player speaker. *"You killed him. Why?"*

And then we all listened to Dennis's confession: *"I thought you might wimp out. I couldn't take that chance. So I did it. But the police will think you did it. Everyone will think you did it."*

An officer moved to grab Dennis. But Dennis made no attempt to run. He stood with his head bowed, his black hair falling down over his face.

"The charge will be assault with intent to kill," an officer was saying.

Caitlin was crying for real now. A policeman recited her rights to her in a low monotone.

I heard a loud siren out front. I knew it was the ambulance for Mr. Northwood.

The officer let go of my arms. He apologized. "We'll

need your statement, but you can give it later," he said softly.

He gestured to Dennis and Caitlin and frowned. "Some friends you got," he said sarcastically. "I never heard of anything like this. What was that he was saying on the tape about a dare?"

I watched the officers guide Dennis and Caitlin to the police cruisers. Caitlin was sobbing loudly. Dennis walked with his head bowed.

"The dare? It was all just a fantasy," I told him. "Just a crazy fantasy that got too real."

I turned away from the flashing red lights and hurried to my house.

About the Author

"Where do you get your ideas?"

That's the question that R. L. Stine is asked most often. "I don't know where my ideas come from," he says. "But I do know that I have a lot more scary stories in my mind that I can't wait to write."

So far, he has written nearly three dozen mysteries and thrillers for young people, all of them bestsellers.

Bob grew up in Columbus, Ohio. Today he lives in an apartment near Central Park in New York City with his wife, Jane, and thirteen-year-old son, Matt.

The Nightmares Never End . . .
When You Visit

NEXT: *BAD DREAMS*

The horrible dreams seem so real to poor Maggie Travers. Night after night she must witness the same gruesome murder. The victim cries out for help, but Maggie always wakes up before she can identify the attacker. And then the terrifying accidents begin. Is the dream a warning? Maggie must force herself to finish the dream . . . before her entire life becomes a nightmare!